FIRST

DOROTHY CORK

MILLS & BOON LIMITED
15–16 BROOK'S MEWS
LONDON W1A 1DR

All the characters in this book have no existence outside the imagination of the Author, and have no relation whatsoever to anyone bearing the same name or names. They are not even distantly inspired by any individual known or unknown to the Author, and all the incidents are pure invention.

The text of this publication or any part thereof may not be reproduced or transmitted in any form or by any means, electronic or mechanical, including photocopying, recording, storage in an information retrieval system, or otherwise, without the written permission of the publisher.

This book is sold subject to the condition that it shall not, by way of trade or otherwise, be lent, resold, hired out or otherwise circulated without the prior consent of the publisher in any form of binding or cover other than that in which it is published and without a similar condition including this condition being imposed on the subsequent purchaser.

*First published 1980
Australian copyright 1980
Philippine copyright 1981
This edition 1981*

© Dorothy Cork 1980

ISBN 0 263 73425 0

*Made and printed in Great Britain by
Richard Clay (The Chaucer Press) Ltd, Bungay,
Suffolk*

CHAPTER ONE

FIVE-FIFTEEN. Fay Douglas glanced at her watch and sighed. She was tired, really tired, and the heavy perfume of flowers that still lingered in the shop made her head ache. This was her first day back at work after a bout of summer 'flu, and though her boss, Mrs Markham, had taken pity on her and was doing the cleaning up in the back room that was usually her job, she still had to stay on till five-thirty, to attend to any last-minute customers.

Fay, perched on a tall white stool, smoothed down the skirt of her pale green and white floral overall. If nobody bought the last of the red roses, she would buy them herself—a mad extravagance, but right now she felt in need of something to cheer her up. The prospect of going home to an empty apartment was not a cheerful one.

She sighed again and ran a hand through her hair, a little surprised as she rediscovered its shortness. She had worn it shoulder-length for years, but had it cut and restyled for the wedding. Walter Marshall, her stepfather-to-be, had suggested it, and had also given her the money—and the very day after she had had it done she had developed 'flu, with the result that she hadn't even gone to the wedding.

She looked at her watch again, elegant, gold, with a smooth band that fitted her wrist perfectly. Walter had given her that too. She certainly had acquired the nicest stepfather who ever lived, and she had no doubts that he would make her mother, Claire, very happy. But just now she did wish, rather selfishly, that Claire could have been there when she went home tonight. Instead, she and Walter had set off on a tour of the world, and wouldn't be back to Australia for at least four months—depending on how Walter, who was sixty and not in the very best of health, was standing up to the pace. A little wistfully, and knowing it was a terribly naïve thought, Fay wished she could have gone along too. It was funny, really. She was the one who had been saving up for a trip overseas, with a girl friend, ever since she had left school three years ago. Her mother spent every penny of her income, and gave scarcely a thought to tomorrow, yet she was the one who was taking a trip.

Well, good luck to her, Fay thought. She slid quickly off the stool as two people came into the shop—a handsome man and a fair-haired girl. Good lord! Her cornflower-blue eyes widened. It was her stepsister!

'Sondra!' she exclaimed, moving forward to meet her. 'How lovely to see you! Did you want some flowers, or did you just come to see me?' Her voice trailed off uncertainly. Sondra wasn't looking exactly ecstatic about seeing her, even though she must have come here deliberately, knowing very well Fay worked here. She bit her lip as the other girl's grey-green eyes moved over her, and she knew she looked tired and unattractive and that her overall was crumpled. She was well aware that her life was very different from Sondra Marshall's. She was a working girl, while Sondra—well, she had money to burn. Her cream silk Chanel-type suit had probably cost a packet, and everything about her—smooth blonde hair, subtle make-up, manicured fingernails, beautiful shoes—whispered a discreet though perfectly audible 'Money'.

And the man with her—he was expensive-looking too. Fay glanced at him quickly and blinked. Heavens! Did men as handsome as that really exist? He positively had to be a movie actor or a TV star. That golden hair—those blue eyes—that tanned skin! That smile! He wore immaculate white pants and a white jacket of heavy textured cotton, half its buttons undone to reveal a golden chest.

With an effort Fay switched her attention to Sondra to hear her coolly drawled, 'No, I don't want any flowers, Fay. This is my new stepsister, by the way, Tony,' she broke off to tell the man beside her, though she made no attempt at an introduction. 'We've barely met, but now we're related.' She turned back to Fay. 'I dropped in to see what you're up to—if you're still working here. I suppose you have thoughts of opting out of work now.'

'Me?' Fay flushed. 'No—why should I?' She had realised Sondra didn't like her much when they had met for the first and only time some weeks ago—over the dinner at which her mother and Sondra's father broke the news that they were going to marry. Sondra hadn't been pleased about that, either. And now she hadn't even asked if Fay had recovered from the illness that had kept her away from the wedding. It was a pity if they couldn't be friends. Sondra was only three or four years older than herself, though in worldly wisdom and sophistication, Fay thought wryly, her stepsister could probably give her a good ten years.

Sondra was staring at her with a look of cynical amusement on her face, and Fay said nervously, 'Oh, I guess my mother told you I'd been saving for a trip overseas with Dodie Hayes. But just now—well, Walter—your father—they want me to look after the apartment.'

Sondra's delicately darkened eyebrows shot up. 'Oh dear, how noble of you to be so self-sacrificing when you could be darting off to foreign parts.' She took a few graceful steps across the shop, her silk skirt swishing faintly, and paused to pull a carnation from a bunch and sniff at it. Fay caught Tony's eye, and unexpectedly he smiled at her. Such a friendly, stunning smile! Her heart began to hammer as she smiled back, then wondered if she should have, if Sondra mightn't like it. She had turned away and was taking the red roses from their bucket when Sondra wandered back to say briskly, 'I'll be in to take a look around the apartment some evening, by the way. If you happen to have a spare key with you, you can give it to me.'

'I'm afraid I haven't,' said Fay, a little taken aback—because surely the apartment was nothing to do with Sondra.

'Then hunt one out,' Sondra said. 'Or failing that, have another one cut. I shall want it.'

Fay bit her lip. No reason, no please, and after all, the flat was *her* home, even though she had had an argument with Claire about it, because she would have preferred somewhere smaller, less pretentious. Sondra, as far as she knew, still lived in Queanbeyan, in her father's house.

Without answering the other girl, she laid the red roses on a sheet of pale green oiled paper and carefully wrapped their stems, then reached for green tissue. It was five-thirty and in a minute Mrs Markham would be coming out to lock up.

'If those roses are for me,' said Sondra, 'forget it. I have a dinner date in Canberra before I drive home, and we have lashings of flowers in the garden there. Shop flowers don't mean a thing to me.'

Fay flushed. It wasn't going to improve their relationship to tell Sondra that the roses weren't for her, but she felt angry at her stepsister's unmistakable rudeness. What must Tony, with his friendly smile, be thinking? He must be listening to the conversation, even though he was taking no part in it. She wondered what

Sondra would tell him about her over their dinner date. Lucky Sondra! Dinner with a stunning man like that had never come Fay's way. Any dreams she might have had about a handsome man coming to the flower shop and falling in love with her had never come true. But then there was nothing glamorous about her, with her small pale face and unexciting brown hair. The new hair-style had made a difference, but a week in bed with 'flu had hardly enhanced her appearance.

'Remember,' added Sondra, 'I'll be in to see the apartment and check what you're doing with it. It belongs to my father, even if you think otherwise.'

Fay put the money for the roses in the cash register and said evenly, 'You'll let me know when you're coming, won't you, Sondra?'

'Why? Am I likely to catch you entertaining your boy-friend there?'

Fay clenched her teeth and hung on to her self-control. 'I merely meant that if I knew when to expect you then I could be sure of having enough dinner for two,' she said as coolly as she could manage.

'I'll take a chance on that,' answered Sondra.

Mrs Markham had appeared by now, obviously to close the shop, and without a word of goodbye Sondra swept out. The man with her, Tony, raised his hand in a little salute to Fay and followed her.

'What about these roses?' Mrs Markham, a woman in her early fifties, frowningly indicated the wrapped flowers. 'Was there some argument that they didn't take them?'

'I wrapped them for myself,' Fay explained. 'I—I put the money in the cash register, Mrs Markham.'

Mrs Markham gave her a rather sharp smile. 'I suppose you can afford treats like that nowadays,' she remarked dryly, and Fay flushed at her tone. 'Those two people were friends of yours, I suppose. All that chatter that was going on——'

'It was my stepsister, as a matter of fact,' Fay said quietly.

'Oh? Very smart-looking, isn't she—and her boyfriend too. Well, I hope they're not going to make a habit of calling in and distracting you from your work ... Next thing we'll see *you* wearing model suits and lunching in the best restaurants. Perhaps I should have kept Judy on—you're probably thinking of giving up work now.'

'Oh no, Mrs Markham,' Fay said quickly. Judy James was the girl who had been temporarily employed while she was away with 'flu. 'I'm still—my mother's marriage hasn't made the least difference to me. It's not as if I were a schoolgirl and would have to be dependent on them.'

Mrs Markham smiled slightly. 'Oh, dear me, Fay, your mother's marriage has made a lot of difference to you already. For a start, you've moved out of that poky little apartment into something rather more sumptuous, haven't you? You told me all about it three or four weeks ago.'

Fay flushed. 'Yes, but—well, it's just because my stepfather happens to own that apartment block and there was a unit vacant. It's not as if there's rent to pay, and he wants a base in Canberra. I mean, if my mother does any more books she'll want to come in to the National University for research, so you see I'm really just looking after the flat till they come back.'

Mrs Markham raised her eyebrows. 'Spare me the explanations, Fay. I think we've established that life has changed for you. Why, you even look different. That new hair-style has changed you almost beyond recognition.' Her eyes skimmed over Fay in a way that was not altogether friendly. 'And your little gold watch—where did that come from? Your stepfather?'

Fay bit her lip. Mrs Markham was right, of course. Her life had changed. But not all that much. 'Yes,' she said. 'It was a gift. He's very generous.' She didn't mention the five thousand dollars Walter had put into an account for her, and that she meant only to use for expenses connected with the flat. 'But whatever you think, I want to be independent. I won't be living with them—part of the family.' And what's more, she thought a little wryly, her new stepsister wouldn't like it, probably wouldn't tolerate it.

'Well, we shall see,' shrugged Mrs Markham. 'When money's available—money and the privileges of the wealthy—it's a great temptation.'

Fay didn't comment. She was happy as she was, and that was that. She went to change out of her overall and to fetch her handbag, and a few minutes later she and her employer had left the shop and gone their separate ways in the warm summer evening.

Fay had driven to work today for the first time. The Gemini, only two years old and one of her mother's extravagances, was hers now. Walter was giving Claire a new car when they came back home. As Fay made her way to the parking area a block away, she was conscious that her headache had worsened since her encounter with Sondra. What did she mean, that she was coming to check what she was doing with the apartment? Did she really think she entertained boy-friends there? The fact was, she didn't even have a boy-friend, and had never been in love in her life. The only man who was likely to come to the apartment was Dain Legend, whom her mother had asked to be a sort of guardian while she was away. She thought of him now uneasily. He was divorced, terribly worldly, and as far as she was concerned disturbingly intimidating. She had only met him a couple of times, and that was weeks ago when he had come back to the flat with her mother after they had dined together. Fay had made coffee for them, and he and Claire had talked almost exclusively, as far as Fay knew, of the research her mother was doing for her current book. He had ignored Fay almost completely, all his attention being given to Claire, who was both beautiful and clever, in contrast with Fay—small and unremarkable, and inclined to hide behind her long straightish brown hair. She had wondered at the time if he and Claire were attracted to each other, and she had hoped not. For one thing, her mother was forty-six and he was probably ten or twelve years younger. For another, Fay just didn't like him. He was so darkly brooding, he looked somehow as if he had already experienced the whole of life. His mouth was wide and almost ugly—sensual, even cruel, she thought—and the expression in his practically black eyes, on the few occasions when she happened to meet his gaze, had sent shivers down her spine.

It had come as a complete surprise—as a shock, rather—when a few days before the wedding her mother told her she wanted Dain Legend to keep an eye on her, and to help her if she should be in need of advice.

'But, Mother, why?' she had exclaimed. 'I won't need any advice—I'll just be doing the same old things. I can look after myself—you know I can. I'll only be a nuisance to him, and he—well, I don't *know* him, I—I just don't like him. Please, don't ask him!'

'Too late, dear,' Claire had said, unperturbed. 'I've already put it to him and he's agreed. I've also more or less promised you'll do some typing for him, since you won't be busy with mine.'

'What?' Fay stared at her uncomprehendingly. 'Why should he want typing done? He's a sheep farmer!'

'Fay, don't you ever listen to anything? Don't you know what we were discussing those evenings when he came here?'

'Your book,' Fay said promptly. Her mother had taken honours in Sociology at the University while her husband, a lecturer in English, had still been alive. Since then she had written several studies, the current one dealing with women's liberation concepts in rural Australia of the nineteenth century—a work that was being held over until she came back from her world tour. Fay did her typing for her and, secretly, often found it rather heavy going, so that she was quite looking forward to the break.

'Yes, my book, of course,' Claire said a trifle impatiently. 'But why do you think such a topic should be of any interest to Dain?'

'I have no idea,' Fay admitted. Truth to tell, she hadn't even given it a thought. Her mother had several intellectual friends with whom Fay had little in common, some of them young, some middle-aged. She had just accepted Dain Legend as one of them, except that for some reason his very presence seemed to rub her up the wrong way.

'Well, he's been getting together a history of his sheep station, Legend's Run,' Claire told her, 'and so our research overlapped to some extent. In fact, he's been able to help me quite considerably in some directions. Now he's reached the stage of needing a typist, and naturally I suggested you. It's a way of repaying him for the invaluable help he's given me.'

Fay sighed. 'You might have mentioned it to me first. I don't really want to do any more typing just now.'

Claire raised her eyebrows. 'I have no doubt he'll insist on paying you for it, dear. He's not the kind of man to use you. Or don't you feel there's any need to save up for your trip now I'm marrying Walter?' she added shrewdly.

Fay flushed. 'Of course I do. But—oh well, what's

the use? It's done now, I suppose, and I'll just have to make the best of it. When am I supposed to start?'

'Certainly not until after the wedding. Dain's gone to Melbourne—to visit his ex-wife, I believe. But the minute he comes back he's promised to call in and see how you're coping. After all, you're very young, and you've never been on your own.'

Great, Fay thought, her heart sinking. She felt trapped, but forced herself not to utter any further protests, though she couldn't resist remarking, 'I'm surprised he's visiting his ex-wife. I thought you said he was well rid of her—that she was probably unfaithful to him.'

'Well, one hears things, and I do think that's the case.' Claire leaned back in the sage green velvet armchair, part of the new suite Walter had bought for the sitting room, and smoothed one hand over her lovely auburn hair. 'As for why he's visiting her, I didn't ask him.'

'Perhaps he's still in love with her,' Fay suggested, and her mother laughed aloud.

'My dear, are you trying to make a romantic of Dain Legend? I assure you a man who's still sentimentally in love with the woman he's divorced from doesn't look at other women the way he does. At me—at you. He couldn't be more cynical. It's a great shame, really. He's too admirable a specimen of the human male to spend the rest of his life alone. And who knows, he might get back a little of his faith in women while he's taking an interest in you. You're such a good, wholesome child.'

Fay was speechless. Her mother wasn't by any chance suggesting that Dain Legend might fall in love with *her*, was she? That would be absolutely ludicrous. In fact, it almost sent her into fits. She only hoped she didn't suspect her mother's motives...

Now as she reached the car park and headed for the

Gemini, she told herself she would somehow or other get out of doing that typing for him. Then he wouldn't have any good excuse for seeing her. He would probably be glad enough not to have to bother about her, anyway. She unlocked the door of the car and had just deposited her bunch of roses on the passenger seat when a man's voice said, 'Fay——'

She straightened and turned quickly and nearly fell over with shock. It was the man who had been with Sondra—that stunningly good-looking man she had called Tony. Fay stared at him, feeling the colour flood into her pale cheeks. What on earth was he doing here in the car park? Shouldn't he be with Sondra, having a pre-dinner drink somewhere in town?

She swallowed and tried to think of something to say, but nothing came.

'Don't look at me like that,' he said, laughing. 'I assure you my intentions are strictly honourable. I didn't get a chance to talk to you in the florists, so I waited till you came out and followed you. My name's Tony Thorpe, by the way—and you're Fay.'

'Yes. Fay Douglas,' she said uncertainly. 'What—what did you want to talk to me about?'

'Well, to begin with—what are you doing tonight? Do you have a date?'

She shook her head. 'I'm going home, that's all. I've just got over 'flu and I'm rather tired.'

He looked rueful. 'I'm sorry. I was going to ask you to have dinner with me. I'm down from Queensland for a couple of months to have another look around the A.C.T., and I don't really know all that many people here.'

'Oh. I—I thought you were having dinner with Sondra,' said Fay. Her legs felt weak. This couldn't be happening to Fay Douglas! A man who looked like Tony Thorpe couldn't possibly want to take *her* out to dinner.

'Sondra has something else lined up,' he said. 'Look, why don't we get into your car? I can't keep you standing here when you're feeling crook.' He held the door open for her while she slid in behind the wheel, then walked round and took the seat beside her. 'If you're wondering whether you should go out with me because of Sondra, then stop wondering. She met me this afternoon for old times' sake and that's all.' It was exactly what Fay had been wondering, and she was relieved. 'I met her a year ago, here in Canberra,' Tony continued, looking at her seriously. 'We saw quite a bit of each other and I'll admit she was one reason why I came back again. But we'vve both changed. Or maybe we just see each other differently. The thing's gone cold anyhow, and this afternoon proved it. So here I am, at a loose end, and—at the risk of sounding corny—when you looked at me and smiled in the shop just now, my heart went bang. So if you don't feel like coming out tonight, then how about tomorrow?'

'I'd love it,' smiled Fay. She still couldn't believe it. His heart had gone bang when she smiled at him! No one had ever said anything like that to her before. And had he any idea what *her* heart had done when he smiled at her? Impulsively she said, 'If you like, we could have something to eat in my apartment tonight.'

'Do you mean that? It wouldn't be imposing on you?'

'No, honestly, I'd like it. There's steak in the freezer,' she remembered.

'That sounds great. Where do you live?'

'Ainslie,' she said, and he smiled.

'Better than ever. I'm in a motel in the same area. But I promise not to stay late—you'll want to get to bed early.'

She nodded gratefully. 'I'm afraid so.' She started up the car and in minutes they were floating up Northbourne Avenue—or that was how it felt to Fay. This was like a dream, it was wonderful, and yet another side of her was anxious. There had to be something wrong somewhere, this sort of thing just couldn't happen to her.

They had a lovely evening. Her headache vanished completely. Tony helped her with the steak and vegetables and she couldn't help feeling glad she had this lovely flat. Thanks to Walter. Tony even helped her wash the dishes, and meanwhile she learned that he was a jackeroo on his father's big cattle station in western Queensland. At this time of year, he had two or three months' holiday because they couldn't work the cattle till the Wet was over. When he went back, he told her, he was to manage the outstation.

'I reckoned on coming down to see Sondra and then take it from there,' he admitted, 'but as I told you, she and I just don't click any more. Actually I was beginning to play with the idea of whizzing off to France for two or three weeks.'

Fay listened, her blue eyes wide. Imagine having enough money to be able to think like that! Privately, she hoped he wouldn't disappear to France, but she didn't dare say it aloud.

The kitchen tidied, they went into the sitting room, and with soft music playing on the radio, and the lights low, they talked some more, and the subject of her mother's marriage to Walter Marshall came up.

'I rather gathered you and Sondra aren't close friends,' he remarked, and Fay grimaced.

'We don't really know each other. But I guess she's a little resentful at having her life changed so drastically—you know, another woman moving into the house.'

'Your life must have changed too,' he suggested. 'How do you get on with your stepfather?'

'Oh, marvellously,' she said enthusiastically. 'He's a darling, and just incredibly generous. I don't intend living with them when they come back, though.'

'You'll stay on in this flat?'

'I don't think so. Only while they're away—as a sort of caretaker. Walter's put in new carpets and furniture and it should be looked after. He put a crazy amount of money in my bank account too, so I won't have any money problems if there are any emergencies. I'm really just so lucky to have a stepfather like him.'

'And I'm lucky to have run into a girl like you,' said Tony, moving closer to her on the sofa.

The next minute she was in his arms and he was kissing her, not in the least demandingly, but very thoroughly, so she was breathless when he let her go.

'Oh lord, I didn't mean to do that,' he said with a laugh. 'I hope you're not angry?'

She shook her head, half her mind still marvelling that this should be happening to her. Her cheeks were flushed and her eyes starry. 'No, of course I'm not angry, Tony—but——'

'But you think that's enough? You're right, of course.' He took hold of her hand and began to play with her fingers. 'I promised I wouldn't stay late, so I shan't. I'll go now, and let you get to bed. But don't forget tomorrow night—I'm taking you out to dinner ... Have a good night's sleep, Fay, and thanks a lot for letting me come here.'

She smiled again. She didn't want him to go so soon, but she knew it would be wise—and she knew that when he had gone, and she lay in bed, she would go over every single thing they had said to each other.

'I'll pick you up here at seven-thirty,' he suggested, as they went into the wide front hall. 'That should give you time to come home and change, shouldn't it?'

Fay nodded and opened the door for him.

'Goodnight,' he said, then took her into his arms for a moment, kissing her softly on the lips and ruffling her hair.

It was as they drew apart that Fay realised someone had come up in the elevator and was standing no more than two feet from the doorway. She felt herself go scarlet. It was Dain Legend.

He wore black trousers and a black collarless shirt with a wine-coloured cravat at the neck, and he looked darkly menacing. There was an odd expression on his face as his narrowed eyes met hers, and after an instant she realised he didn't recognise her. It was her hair, of course. The new cut had changed her appearance considerably. It feathered softly over her forehead and her ears, and curved in gracefully to the back of her head. The hairdresser had said it emphasised her good bone structure and made the most of her heart-shaped face.

Fay was suddenly amused. She had given this man who had completely ignored her in the past a distinct surprise, and it gave her confidence. With one hand on Tony's arm she said brightly, 'Don't you recognise me, Mr Legend? You are looking for me, aren't you? I'm Fay Douglas.'

His lips curved in a grim smile. 'I'd just begun to realise that ... Yes, I'm looking for you, Fay Douglas, and I want to talk to you. Have you quite finished your farewells?'

Oh dear—that tone of voice! Well, if he had been under the impression she was a child when he had agreed to keep an eye on her, then he would have to do some rethinking. She wasn't a child, and she wasn't in need of a guardian, and if they were going to have a talk, she would very quickly acquaint him of the fact. Meanwhile she had better do the conventional thing and introduce him to Tony.

'Tony, this is a friend of my mother's, Mr Legend.

Mr Legend—Tony Thorpe.'

Dain Legend's eyes assessed the younger man as he remarked coldly, 'I believe we met a year or so ago, at the theatre. You were with Sondra Marshall.'

'Could be,' Tony agreed, looking surprised. Fay looked surprised too. She hadn't realised Dain Legend knew her stepsister. Tony had turned back to her. 'Shall I go, Fay? Or do you want me to stay?'

Fay's eyes widened. Was he possibly suggesting she mightn't be safe with Dain Legend? That was quite funny. She was in no danger from him, except that she was going to have an argument with him about his— supervisory duties. Though for all she knew, he might be relieved to be rid of her. 'It's okay,' she told Tony.

'Then I'll see you tomorrow.' With a brief and polite goodnight to the older man, he made his way to the elevator.

Without being asked, Dain Legend stepped inside the hall and closed the door firmly, and after a second Fay, her confidence slightly shaken, led the way to the sitting room—with its low lights, soft music, and crumpled cushions on the sofa. In their bowl on the table, the red roses, that she had put in water while the steak was cooking, made a bright splash of colour.

She turned to face him and said coolly, her head up, 'Isn't this a rather funny sort of hour to be calling?'

He raised his dark eyebrows. 'I saw your light, and assuming you'd be at work tomorrow, I thought I'd call now. Nine-thirty's hardly late, is it?'

He stood looking down at her and she remembered what Claire had said. 'A man who's sentimentally in love doesn't look at women the way he does.' Her tongue came out to moisten her upper lip nervously, and she felt a shiver run down her spine. What did the expression in his eyes mean? They were so dark they were almost black, and totally unreadable. After a moment they released her own eyes and went to her short-cut hair, then travelled down over her slim body. She was still wearing the pale blue sleeveless shirtmaker dress she had worn home from work, and her hand strayed nervously to the top buttons to check if they were fastened.

'Yes,' he said looking at her cynically from under his black brows, 'they're all done up, though certainly you look more than a little crumpled.' His mouth curved cruelly and she felt her own lips tremble as she tried to think of some clever retort. It was hopeless, of course, and she was relieved when he asked abruptly, 'May I sit down?'

'Do,' she said, equally abruptly. He took one end of the sofa and she sat in an armchair a little away from him. 'I'd appreciate it if you'd let me know you were coming.'

'I imagine you would,' he drawled. 'However, it didn't occur to me. Your mother told me you were a—sheltered, wholesome, stay-at-home child, I think that was how she put it. And as I remembered you, with your hair hanging down your back and a tendency to be scarcely more seen than heard, I had no reason to imagine you otherwise.'

'Really?' Her cheeks were scarlet again. 'And now have I done something frightful?'

'You know the answer to that better than I do,' he said maddeningly. 'I can only judge by your guilty looks. But it seems to have taken you no time at all to graduate to entertaining men in this flat.'

Entertaining men! The blood came hotly to Fay's cheeks. 'You—you must be off your head!' she stammered out furiously. 'Do you think just—having a friend to dinner is—immoral or something? Especially as he left at half past nine—which *you* seem to think is a perfectly respectable hour to *begin* a visit.'

'A visit with a somewhat different purpose,' he retorted. 'How long have you known Tony Thorpe?'

'Not long,' she said, her head up. 'But he's—he's a friend of Sondra's.'

'I hardly think he's a close friend. An acquaintance, perhaps. How did you come to meet him?'

'Through Sondra. How would you imagine?' she said icily. 'Anyhow, what do you want to talk to me about that's so important? I want to go to bed. I've only just got up from an attack of 'flu.'

'Just as well,' he commented sardonically. 'Otherwise your visitor might have stayed—longer.'

Fay sighed exaggeratedly. 'Honestly, the way you keep harping on that theme's beginning to bore me! I may as well tell you I didn't want my mother to ask you to—to poke your nose into my affairs in the first place, and if you're going to be so officious, I'd rather you didn't come here. If I need any advice from you I can ask for it. But I think it's very unlikely.'

He stretched one arm along the back of the sofa, and as he moved the light glinted on the thick black hair at his temple. 'I'm going to give you some advice whether you ask for it or not, Fay. As for your wants, I'm not remotely interested in them. I agreed to act as your guardian and I'm not going back on my word, however distasteful to myself or boring to you ... Here's my first bit of advice, and I hope you'll take it. Quit entertaining men in your apartment—and drop Tony Thorpe.'

Fay looked at him incredulously. 'Do you really think you have the right to choose my friends for me? We—we don't even know each other! Up till now we've scarcely exchanged a word. If you think I'm going to put up with having *you* tell me what to do or what not to do, then——'

'Then I'm mistaken, is that it?' he interrupted, his

mouth curving unpleasantly. 'My God, it's as well your mother did ask me to look in on you now and again. What's your big idea now she's not at hand to supervise you? To whoop it up? To get yourself into a load of trouble?'

'I'm not getting myself into a load of trouble,' she retorted. 'But what's the use of talking to someone like you? You seem to have a one-track mind!'

'You mean,' he said studying her for a long unnerving minute, 'that I think you're in danger of losing your virtue? Well, you're damned right, that's exactly what I think. What's more, you must know very well I'm not the only male with a one-track mind. How about your friend Tony? What was he doing here tonight?'

'We—we had dinner and talked,' Fay said angrily. 'And then he—kissed me goodnight at the door.'

'Yes? And before that—in here on the sofa?' he said crudely, and despite herself she coloured. Yet Tony had done no more than kiss her and she—she hated Dain Legend for his nasty suspicions.

'I'm not going to discuss Tony with you,' she said, her head up. 'I'm nearly twenty, and I know what I'm doing.'

'I doubt it,' he broke in. 'If you have any sense, you'll accept my authority and do as I tell you.'

'I won't!' she exclaimed, her cornflower-blue eyes stormy. 'I'm not one of your stupid sheep to be rounded up and pushed through a gate into some paddock——'

'You want to frisk around with the rams, do you?' he said with a cynical smile, and she gave an exclamation of disgust.

'Next thing you'll be telling me where that leads to. You can save your breath. I'm not the sort of girl you seem to imagine.'

'A few more steps in the wrong direction and you will

be,' he drawled. 'Don't you even know when you're taking a risk?' He got up from the sofa as he spoke and came to sit on the arm of her chair. She edged away, but he leaned over and gripped her by the chin, forcing her to look at him. 'I didn't recognise you when I saw you tonight. When did you get your image restyled? That's certainly a cunning hairdo—it's done all sorts of things for you, including showing off your tiptilted nose and those wide blue eyes. As for your mouth—other times I've met you you've kept it shut, but right now I find it very, very tempting——'

Fay pulled away from him, her heart beating hard. It was the look in his eyes that alarmed her most. 'Leave me alone,' she said huskily. 'I had my hair cut for the wedding, then I had 'flu——'

'You didn't get to the wedding?' He was laughing at her, his lips curving sensually. 'You mean today's the first time you've ventured out since you've had your looks updated?'

'If you want to put it that way—yes.' She had got to her feet and moved away from him. In a minute she would either burst into tears or shout at him. She decided to shout. 'Now will you please go away—and don't come back again. I don't like you and I won't let you in.'

'You're a rude little brat,' he told her, getting up from the chair indolently. 'You're also dangerously attractive. I don't know whether I should beat you or kiss you, and I'm tempted to do both.'

'I'm not going to let you do either,' she snapped, though her heart was hammering with fright. 'And if you try to touch me I'll—I'll——'

'Oh, calm down,' he said irritably. 'You're in no danger. For God's sake sit down and stop shouting and look at a few simple facts for a change.' As he spoke he flung himself down on the sofa again, and after a minute Fay resumed her seat in the armchair, but tensely, and acutely aware that she really had no alternative.

'Believe me, I came here tonight with the best of intentions,' Dain said then. 'After all, you've been left on your own, and my image of you was of a rather introverted and decidedly immature kid who hadn't been around—that's the impression you gave me the few times we met, anyhow. Add to that the fact your mother felt you needed a guardian—a protector—and you get the general picture of how I thought of you.' He paused, and Fay didn't look at him. She linked her fingers together and unlinked them, and said nothing.

'So then I get here and find you in the middle of a goodnight kiss and looking nothing like the quiet little homebody who was going to do some typing for me. Looking in fact very provocative and acting so guilty I wondered if you'd just had an hour in bed with your boy-friend.'

Fay looked up. That was just too much, and she burst out furiously, 'You *do* have a nasty mind, Mr Legend! You're just so cynical you suspect the worst for no reason at all.'

His lips twisted. 'I apologise. I'll accept that you haven't been to bed with Tony Thorpe. Not yet. As for my cynicism, I'm a realist. I know that Nature can make some very fast moves.'

'And what's that supposed to mean?'

'Well, let's see—that once the fires of passion are lit they're hard to control. You'll understand what I mean if you've ever seen a bushfire. Do I make myself plain? Or am I boring you again?'

'Yes, you are, Mr Legend,' Fay snapped angrily. 'I'm just an ordinary normal girl, and Tony Thorpe happens to be a—a gentleman. *Those* are simple facts, if that's what you want.'

He viewed her levelly, then one eyebrow tilted. 'As you see them,' he said, and shifted his position slightly—and with it, the topic of conversation. 'Now about the typing you're going to do for me——'

'You're not going to hold me to that!' she exclaimed. 'Knowing how I feel——'

'I don't particularly care how you feel. But it might help to keep you occupied in the evenings, and it will suit me very well.'

'I can't see why, when you live the other side of Queanbeyan. You could easily find a typist there.'

'I can see you're not well informed, Fay,' he drawled. 'I come to Canberra frequently and in fact I have an apartment on the top floor here.'

'Here?' she gasped.

'Why not? That's how I came to see your light when I came in tonight. I have a feeling I'll be spending quite a bit of my time here during the next few weeks.'

'While your sheep station runs itself, I suppose,' she said scornfully.

'I have a manager. And unless it rains we're not all that busy just now.' For the second time he got up. 'I'll let you get to bed now, Fay, and I hope what I've said will sink well into your consciousness. I'm going to take my responsibility for you seriously, whether you like it or not. So—no more men in the apartment.'

'That's a ridiculous restriction. It's—it's prehistoric! My mother never meant you to treat me as though I were a schoolgirl,' she added, leaning back in the chair now, and curling her feet under her. Her eyes met his challengingly, and he paused and stood still, looking back at her.

'What are you trying to do now, looking at me like that?' he said softly. 'Show me you're not a schoolgirl? Tempting me to——' He stopped, narrowing his eyes.

'To—to what?' she asked, her heart suddenly beating

fast.

'To do what most men would do. And if you pretend ignorance, then so help me I'll do it—if only to teach you a lesson, Miss Douglas.'

Fay swallowed and turned her face away from him. She had a feeling of complete helplessness. It had never entered her head that she was taking any sort of a chance when she invited Tony Thorpe here to dinner, but now, alone with Dain Legend, it was a very different matter. He was a considerably bigger man than Tony, older, and without Tony's charm or fabulously good looks. But he had charisma. She was strongly aware of it. Aware too of his intense masculinity. The fact was, she wasn't used to men and his presence unnerved her. She knew she should get up now and see him to the door, but she was afraid to do so in case he should—well, what *was* she afraid he might do? he wasn't likely to kiss her—or to beat her either. He was—contemptuous of her. He didn't like her any more than she liked him.

'I don't need to be taught a lesson by you,' she said unsteadily. 'Not any sort of lesson. You can see yourself out.'

'I'll do that,' he agreed. 'You can expect to see me again tomorrow.'

'I'll be going out,' she said promptly. 'With Tony. And I don't know what time I'll be home.'

'It doesn't matter. I can wait,' Dain said mockingly.

A minute later she heard the front door click shut.

She stayed where she was for a long moment. Her body was trembling and she was full of inexpressible feelings. Dain Legend had upset her equilibrium badly. She'd been out to defeat him, but she hadn't won. Not yet.

Presently she got up from the chair and went to her bedroom, switching on the light over the mirror and looking at her reflection searchingly. Heavens, she looked a wreck! Her face was deathly pale and there were dark shadows under her eyes. Mentally she compared herself with Sondra, so svelte and composed and elegant. It had been quite a shock to discover that Dain Legend knew her, though she wasn't sure why.

Wearily she undressed, deciding she would shower in the morning. She was too tired now—it had been quite a day. In bed with the light out, she determinedly thought of Tony and the instant attraction they had felt for each other. She thought about his father's cattle station in Queensland. Tomorrow she would ask him to tell her more about that and the work he did there. 'What shall I wear?' she wondered. She had never spent much money on clothes, but Claire sometimes passed on dresses she had tired of, though Fay didn't have occasion to wear many of them.

'I'll take up the hem of the black chiffon,' she thought. Tony was sure to take her somewhere smart, and perhaps they'd go to a disco afterwards—though she would just as soon talk. Unexpectedly her mind switched to the end of the evening—to coming home and finding that man waiting for her. She clenched her teeth in fury. Surely Dain wouldn't have the cheek to wait around for her, to—to check her in. It was ghastly to think he had an apartment in this very building, that right at this minute he was up there somewhere—maybe thinking of her——

She turned on her side and banished him from her thoughts.

CHAPTER TWO

FAY had an extra door key cut during her lunch hour next day. She thought Sondra had a frightful cheek to act the way she had about the apartment, but still they were stepsisters, and she didn't want to antagonise her. It would be nice if they could be friends, but that remained to be seen.

That evening, just as she was leaving the shop, Sondra appeared.

'Have you done anything about that key, Fay?' she demanded at once, and Fay managed a smile.

'Yes, I have an extra one right here. Did you want it now?'

'That was the idea. I'm staying in town and there's no sense in my going to a hotel when there's a flat available.'

'I'll be out for dinner, I'm afraid,' said Fay a little nervously, thinking of Tony and wondering if Sondra would be displeased about the friendship. From what he had said, it shouldn't matter, but just the same she decided to say nothing about him.

'Don't imagine I want to have dinner with you,' Sondra said coldly. 'I have other plans, but naturally I want my own doorkey.'

Fay bit her lip. Her own doorkey—free access to *Fay's* flat. She opened her handbag and produced the key. 'When shall I expect you?'

'When I come in is my own affair,' Sondra said. 'When shall I expect you, come to that?'

Fay flushed at this obvious rudeness. 'I shan't be late. Actually I'm having dinner with Tony Thorpe.' She'd said it after all, and she waited for her stepsister's reaction. The other girl stared at her for a second and then uttered a little laugh.

'Well, well! Someone's a fast worker! I suppose you're congratulating yourself on edging your way into my circle so rapidly. What it is to be Walter Marshall's stepdaughter!'

'That has nothing to do with it,' Fay said swiftly. 'I didn't think Tony was exactly in your circle, anyhow.'

'You're right, he's not. And if you're worried, you needn't be. You have my blessing.'

What did that mean? Fay had no real idea. She couldn't fool herself she felt comfortable with Sondra or enjoyed talking to her. All the time there was this patronising undertone, and she had the very strong impression that Sondra actively disliked her. She glanced at her little gold watch. 'I'll have to go now, Sondra. I want to change.'

'For the great dinner date—of course! I suppose you've been buying yourself some new clothes with some of the money my father handed out to you. I notice you've had a visit to the hairdresser too—the one I go to, I shouldn't wonder. You don't look quite so much like the poor relation as you used to, with your hair hanging down in that dreary way, but I can't say you have much flair when it comes to dress.'

'Maybe not,' Fay retorted, goaded into anger. 'But there's one thing I have that you definitely don't possess, Sondra.'

'Really? And what's that?'

'Manners,' said Fay, her voice shaking, and with that she turned on her heel and hurried off to the car park. She should have held her tongue, of course. In saying what she had, she had merely disproved its truth and brought herself down to the same level as Sondra. Heavens—and Sondra was coming to stay at the apartment!

Her spirits sank. She hoped she wouldn't expect to be waited on. She was used to the service that wealth can buy, of course, whereas Fay was not used to putting herself first. She served the customers in the shop, and at home, she had been the one who did the cooking and the housework, because her mother was the one with the brains, the one who wrote those intellectual books. She didn't know if Sondra's intellect was so superior to hers, she knew only that she was rude, that she was always beautifully dressed and groomed, and that Fay Douglas was definitely not one of her favourite people. Apparently she didn't work—she certainly didn't need to—and she could fend for herself if she came to stay. Fay hoped fervently that it would be just for tonight— just to assert her rights.

As she drove home to Ainslie she reflected that her life was changing very rapidly lately. Anyhow, she was going to enjoy herself tonight. She thought of what Tony had said yesterday—that her smile had made his heart go bang. *That* had nothing to do with her being Walter Marshall's stepdaughter!

In the apartment, she showered, then carefully tidied the bathroom. Sondra wasn't going to be able to pick holes in her personal habits. She had been up early that morning to take up the hem of the chiffon dress, so it was all ready for her to wear tonight. Black, she decided, looking at herself critically in the mirror, suited her. It made her look older and it emphasised her fair skin and showed up her graceful neck—a neck that had been hidden for years by long loose hair. She still looked rather washed out after her illness, and after a moment's thought she went into Claire's room and found blusher, eye-shadow and mascara in the dressing table drawer.

A little colour on her cheekbones worked miracles, and the subtle mauvish eye-shadow and dark mascara gave her appearance a decided touch of glamour. She went back to her own room feeling considerably more self-confident. It was extraordinary how much it helped if you knew you were looking your best, and she knew she did look quite attractive, especially with high-heeled black sandals making her legs seem long and slim. The poor relation had blossomed forth, she thought ironically—and without spending a cent of the money Walter had so generously given her.

She found the little beaded evening purse her mother had given her for her eighteenth birthday, and was ready when Tony arrived. She had checked that everything was in order in case Sondra came home before she did, and she had put bedlinen and bathtowels ready in the third bedroom, though she hadn't made up the bed. Sondra could do that for herself.

Tony looked stunning in a dark suit and white shirt, and her heart beat excitedly at the sight of him. He took her two hands in his and kissed the tip of her nose.

'You look adorable! Was everything all right last night? That guy Dain Legend—I do remember meeting him last year. Is he a friend of yours?'

'I hardly know him,' Fay admitted. 'He's a friend of my mother's really. He's just come back from Melbourne and he looked in to see if I was all right or something.' She decided not to mention that he was her unofficial guardian, but enlarged, 'He wants me to do some work for him—some typing. I type my mother's manuscripts, you see—she writes books on—sociology.' She grimaced humorously. 'And it appears he's writing a book about his sheep station. So——' She spread her hands.

'I hope he's not planning to tie you up,' said Tony. 'I want to see as much of you as I can. You will keep all the time you can free for me, won't you, Fay?' He looked into her eyes as he spoke and she blushed, flattered and still incredulous at his attention.

They went to one of the social clubs and ate in an upstairs restaurant where both service and food were excellent, and afterwards they went in the car he had hired for while he was in Canberra to Regatta Point. They sat in the car looking at the lights in Lake Burley Griffin and the sweep of Commonwealth Avenue Bridge, and he kissed her. It was wonderful, but a little bit worrying too. Fay wasn't sure if she should allow it so unprotestingly. After all, they had only met the day before. It was nothing to do with anything Dain Legend had said to her, she told herself. It was just that she hadn't been around, that was all.

When Tony murmured, 'Shall we go back to your apartment, Fay?' she pulled herself nervously out of his arms.

'No, I—I have to get up early in the morning, Tony. And besides, Sondra will be there.'

'Sondra?' His voice was sharp. 'I thought she just wanted to take a look around, not to stay.'

'Well, she's staying tonight,' Fay told him. 'Maybe a couple of nights. I don't know.' She saw Tony grimace in the darkness.

'In that case, I shan't come in. It sounds as if you too girls are going to get really friendly.'

'I hardly think so,' Fay said honestly. 'But I hope things will improve a bit before our parents come back.'

'I wouldn't worry too much. So long as you get on with your stepfather.'

'Oh, I do. He couldn't be nicer to me.'

'Then that's great. I mean, it will make your mother happy. Well, I guess I'd better see you home. Shall we meet again tomorrow night?'

Fay laughed a little. 'You'll be sick of me! Perhaps we should make it the night after, Tony. I have a few things to catch up on.'

'You're a tease,' he complained. 'Don't play hard to get, Fay.'

'I'm not,' she said, surprised. 'But—every night——'

'I want to see you every night,' Tony told her. 'I wish you didn't have that job, in fact, and then we could meet in the daytime too. Do you promise faithfully to see me the night after next?'

'Yes,' she agreed, her heart fluttering. 'If Sondra's out, we could have dinner at my place again,' she offered, thinking she would show Dain Legend he couldn't order her about.

'I hope she is out,' said Tony. 'Otherwise we'll go to a movie.'

'Fine,' she agreed.

Driving back to the flat she thought of Dain Legend again. He surely wouldn't be waiting for her at this time of night. All the same, she wasn't going to take any chances, and she assured Tony he needn't come up in the elevator with her. Once the doors of the lift had closed, she took her cosmetic mirror from her evening purse and looked at her face quickly. Her hair was a little mussed, and she ran a comb through it, but she didn't bother retouching her lipstick. When the elevator stopped at her floor and the doors glided open, she stepped out with a feeling of nervousness. 'I can wait,' he'd said. But he wasn't there. From the street, she had seen there was no light in the sitting room and that meant that Sondra wasn't home yet, so he couldn't be inside, waiting for her.

She hurried towards the door. She was going to escape him. She would go to bed and put out the lights as quickly as she could. And then, if he should come, he could wait all night. She hoped Sondra wouldn't come back till the early hours of the morning. That would teach *him* a lesson!

She did exactly as she had planned, lighting only the

wall lamp in her room. She stripped off her dress quickly and got into pyjamas, then went barefoot to the bathroom to wash her face and clean her teeth. As she came back into the hallway the doorbell rang loudly and demandingly, and she swore softly beneath her breath, feeling her heart hammering.

Blow him! He could see the light from her bedroom through the skylight over the front door—or else he was gifted with second sight. He rang the bell again, and she suddenly realised with a rush of resentment that he probably thought Tony was there with her. Pressing her lips together, she marched to the door and flung it open. He raked her pyjama-clad figure with one long searing glance, then strode past her into the hall. Fay wanted to laugh. Did he really think Tony was here with her?

He made straight for her room where the light was shining, and she quietly closed the front door and stood with her back to it, full of a sense of triumph, and laughing to herself.

In a moment Dain Legend came striding back to her. He had a cigarette between his lips, and she noticed he was wearing an open-necked tan shirt with the sleeves rolled up above the elbows, and black pants that emphasised the narrowness of his hips. His face was grim and unamused, and his eyes were angry as once again they travelled over her, though this time more slowly. Fay's amusement vanished and she swallowed nervously. No girl could keep her equilibrium when a man looked at her that way. It was as though the animal in him, the cruelty in him, the savage, had taken complete possession. For the first time in her life she became fully aware that she was the female of the species, and she shrank back against the door, listening to the beating of her own heart.

He stopped no more than eighteen inches from her,

and his eyes were on her bosom. She was aware of its rising and falling, and equally aware that its shape was clearly outlined by the soft clinging stuff of her pink pyjamas. Instinctively she crossed her arms to cover her breast, her fingers nervously clinging to her upper arms.

'What's the matter?' she asked, the colour rushing to her face. 'Why—are you looking at me like that?'

'Why do you think?' He took the cigarette from between his lips and crushed it out in a big glass ashtray on the telephone table. 'Because you look—in more ways than one—ready for bed. Just tell me this, will you? Are the pyjamas for my especial benefit?'

'What do you mean?' she stammered. 'I—I didn't know you'd be—here——'

'Quit hunting up excuses. I made it quite plain I'd be here tonight when you came in—and you've obviously chosen to greet me in a state of undress. Naturally I'm wondering if you had it in mind to seduce me.' One corner of his wide mouth quirked upward as he spoke, and his dark eyebrows twisted diabolically.

Fay's heart gave such a leap she thought she was going to die of heart failure. She—seduce him? He must be joking! And she didn't appreciate that kind of a joke. She said huskily, 'I—I was going to bed, that's all. You weren't here when I came in, so——'

'Don't give me that stuff!' He suddenly grabbed her by the wrist, pulling her arms away from her body. 'It strikes me you're a proper little bitch with your great saucer eyes and your quivering chin. I could——' He broke off, jerked her precipitately towards him, then gripped her by both shoulders, pressing his fingers into her soft flesh. 'What do you want?' he asked, staring down into her eyes. 'With your back to the door—barring my exit? Do you think you can play games with me, for God's sake?'

He pulled her pyjama jacket back from one shoulder

as he spoke, and Fay let out a little cry as a button flew off and the curve of breast was exposed.

'I could crush you with one hand,' he muttered through his teeth. 'You'd be helpless ... What are you, anyway? A fool? Or a tart?'

'Neither,' she gasped, her voice little more than a whisper. 'Let go of me! I—I wouldn't have answered the door if you hadn't kept ringing the bell. I didn't want you to come in—I didn't invite you——'

'No, you didn't, did you? But plenty of men don't wait for invitations. Don't you know anything? If not, then you're in danger of finding out too much—too fast.'

His face had come down to hers, and she shrank away from him.

'Under other circumstances,' he gritted, 'I'd take pleasure in teaching you. But I'm supposed to be protecting you, Fay Douglas.' He pressed her shoulders back against the door and she let out a little moan. Her protector! And she was almost terrified out of her wits by him. The V of his unbuttoned shirt was just below the level of her eyes and her gaze was riveted on his tanned skin, the mat of dark hair, and she could smell his maleness.

She said hoarsely, 'My mother must have been out of her mind asking you to look after me——'

'And I must have been out of my mind to agree to it,' he retorted, and suddenly thrusting her roughly aside reached for the door handle. With his fingers already closing round it he told her, 'I'll put my manuscript through your service hatch tomorrow morning before I go back to Legend's Run. You can occupy yourself with that in your spare time and keep out of mischief. And I hope you know now what I mean when I advise you not to ask men to your flat.'

'All men aren't like you,' she said. Some of her composure had returned now that he had let her go. She pulled the top edges of her jacket together. 'You're certainly not coming inside this flat again!'

He didn't answer her but swung the door open, stepped outside, and slammed it shut behind him.

Quivering, distracted, Fay hardly knew what to do. It was madness to be alone in a flat when you were at the mercy of a man like that. And yet she couldn't believe that she was in danger from him. He'd only meant to frighten her, she was sure—and he'd certainly done that! But she resented his suggesting that she had got into her pyjamas for his benefit. On the contrary, she had imagined she would be safe in bed when—or if—he came, and wouldn't even have to speak to him.

She walked down the hall on legs that shook. She needed something to steady her down, and she thought of the cocktail cabinet in the sitting room. Walter had stocked it up for his own benefit—and Claire's. Fay didn't drink, but now she went to the cabinet and poured herself some brandy. With shaking hand she raised the glass to her lips and drank.

It was exactly then she heard the front door open and for a mad moment she thought he had come back. But it was Sondra.

She came into the sitting room dropped down in one of the green velvet chairs and stared at Fay. She was looking unutterably soignée—not a hair out of place. She hadn't been mauled about by whoever had taken her out tonight, Fay reflected dryly. She wore a filmy, floaty dress of off-white with a tracery of delicate flowers on it, and her make-up was immaculate.

Over-conscious of the brandy bottle, of the glass still in her hand, of the button missing from the top of her pyjamas, Fay said shakily, 'Oh, hello, Sondra. I—I wondered when you'd be here. Did you have a nice evening?'

Sondra didn't bother answering. 'Where's Tony?' she asked flatly.

Fay flushed. 'He didn't come in. He's gone back to his motel.'

No comment. Sondra's delicate nostrils quivered. 'What's the brandy in aid of? Or are you in the habit of drinking by yourself—now it's free?' She paused and Fay couldn't think of a thing to say. 'My father's certainly left you a good supply of spirits.'

Her lips dry, Fay said, 'It's not for me. I was just feeling a bit—queasy.'

'Where did you eat?' Sondra asked, but she wasn't interested in getting a reply. She leaned back in the chair and studied her coral pink fingernails and remarked, 'I'd like some coffee.'

Fay swallowed hard. It was one thing to make up your mind you weren't going to run around someone in circles, and it was quite another to tell someone like Sondra that if she wanted coffee then she must get it herself. However, it had to be done.

She set down her glass, moved the brandy bottle back into its place, and closed the cocktail cabinet. Then she told Sondra, 'There's plenty of coffee in the cupboard—instant or fresh, whichever you prefer.'

The two girls looked at each other across the room. Fay's glance didn't waver although her pulses were racing, and she was debating with herself whether or not this was the best way to get on good terms with one's stepsister. Mightn't it possibly be better to do whatever she asked? To show herself eager to please? Maybe—and maybe not. But she wasn't going to do it. It wasn't good for her own morale. Sondra had money, but that didn't mean that Fay Douglas was going to crawl to her. She wanted nothing from Sondra.

Sondra drawled, 'It's really gone to your head, hasn't it, having your mother marry into money. You've really come up in the world.'

'I don't know what you mean,' Fay said after a moment. She was shocked by Sondra's bigheadedness, and it would have been easy to snap back with some rude retort, but something told her she must go carefully. After all, she had claimed earlier today to have good manners—she went on reasonably, 'I don't know how much you know about my family, Sondra, but it may interest you to know that my father was a much respected lecturer at the National University. And my mother's books—even if they don't bring in much money—are very well regarded academically.' She felt her legs weak beneath her but resisted the temptation to sit down. It gave her an advantage to stand, to look down at her stepsister, who was now leaning back in her chair and appeared just slightly disconcerted.

'Money's never been important in my life—or in my mother's,' Fay continued. 'I can't think of her as having married into money, as you put it. That's not what her relationship with your father's based on. Can't you—can't you look at it in a different way and be pleased they've found each other?'

Sondra's lip curled. 'I'm not a romantic and nor am I a nitwit—though you're evidently both. Why should I be pleased that your mother's somehow or other persuaded my father to marry her? He's fifteen years older than she is—he has high blood pressure—he's already had one heart attack. He's obviously wealthy and he's obviously going to die before she does. Do you really imagine I can look at it all as love's young dream? What she's interested in is his money and she's going to get all she can out of him. Look how she's dragged him off on a grand tour of the world! Quite possibly it will kill him—my father! So how can you expect me to be pleased about the set-up? I'm his daughter, and now some rank outsider's making sure she and her daughter—you—come first with him!'

Fay listened in some distress. It honestly hadn't occurred to her that Sondra could feel this way, and she said vehemently, 'You're not being fair! It's not like that at all, Sondra, honestly it's not. I know it's not love's young dream, but my mother does love Walter— very much. She—she's put aside her new book so she can go away with him, and it's he who wants that. You must know that's true.'

'Huh!' Sondra retorted scornfully. 'Do you expect me to believe that's such a sacrifice? She knows what she's doing—*she's* not short of intelligence.'

Fay sighed. 'I'm glad they've married, anyhow,' she said tiredly. She felt just the slightest bit muzzy from the brandy, and she longed to get into bed and go to sleep and forget all about Sondra and her unpleasantness. Dain Legend and Sondra Marshall all in the one evening was really too much to cope with.

'Well, of course you're glad,' Sondra raised her slightly darkened eyebrows and tossed back her gleaming blonde hair. 'That's never been in question. But don't ask me to be glad. As for that woman's loving him—I've said she's intelligent, she's also as cold as a computer. And you may put on that wide-eyed innocent air, but there's lots in it for you too, isn't there? This apartment to start with—plus that great wad of money Daddy put into your bank account while your mother stood by and egged him on. But don't think you're going to walk all over me. I've never been the doormat type. You're merely showing how small-minded you are being miserable about making the coffee. It's a fact I've a right to use this apartment, and if you think you can freeze me out you'll soon find the boot's on the other foot.'

'I have no objection to your using the apartment, Sondra,' Fay assured her. 'Perhaps you'd like to choose which bedroom you want. If so, I'll help you move out anything that belongs to either my mother or myself.'

Sondra glared at her. 'Spare me the humble pie! But I'll certainly suit myself.' She got up and marched out of the room, and Fay felt herself sag. She didn't think Sondra would be difficult about the bedrooms. Her own was the smallest of the three, and the one Claire used was so crammed with her personal belongings it would need a major operation to clear it out. She crossed to the window and looked outside, seeing nothing. She could hear Sondra moving about, and it occurred to her that it could have been very pleasant to share the flat with another girl, it was so big and empty with only herself there. As it was, Sondra's attitude was so aggressive, so disagreeable, it would be like sharing her home with a snake.

Well, she would have to do what she could to improve relations between them, and perhaps in time Sondra would become more friendly. Meanwhile, the four months or so that stretched ahead seemed like an eternity. The only consolation was that Sondra wouldn't be spending all her time in Canberra. There was the house in Queanbeyan, and there, Fay knew from things her mother had said, Sondra would be well taken care of by the housekeeper. Here there would be no cup of tea brought to her when she woke in the morning, no solicitous housekeeper to look after her laundry and her meals.

Presently, and reluctantly, Fay forced herself to move. Sondra was in the spare bedroom struggling with the bedclothes.

'Is everything okay?' Fay asked from the doorway, and Sondra glared at her.

'You might have made this bed up, knowing it would be late when I arrived!'

Fay said nothing. If Sondra had said please, she'd

have helped her make the bed. As it was, she could manage on her own. After a moment she said goodnight and went to her room.

In the morning she slept later than usual, and finding the bathroom empty, showered quickly and dressed before going to the kitchen for a hasty breakfast. Sondra was there already, though she had done nothing about getting breakfast even for herself. In answer to Fay's cheerful good morning, she held out a large envelope with Fay's name on it.

'This was in the service hatch.'

Fay coloured, knowing it must be from Dain Legend.

'It's for you, from Dain Legend,' Sondra continued accusingly, and waited.

Fay could easily have offered no explanation, though quite obviously her stepsister expected one. Like herself, she must be surprised to find that Dain was a mutual acquaintance. After a moment she said pleasantly, 'Oh, you know Mr Legend too, don't you?'

'I know him very well,' said Sondra, perching on a stool and crossing her legs. She wore a sea-green satin kimono beautifully embroidered with flowers, and beneath that were fragile-looking shell pink pyjamas. On her feet, matching the kimono, were embroidered slippers. Though her face was washed clean of make-up, she was still undoubtedly attractive, and her hair shone like gold. 'How do you come to know him, and what on earth is in that packet? Aren't you going to open it?'

'Not yet. I know what it is.' Fay laid it aside and put on the electric kettle. 'Excuse me, Sondra—I want to get at that cupboard.'

Sondra moved fractionally and returned to the fray. 'Exactly when did you meet Dain? I know he's rented a flat here, but he hasn't stayed in Canberra for over a month.'

'Hasn't he?' Fay poured herself some orange juice

from the jug in the fridge. Sondra could get her own breakfast—she wasn't in a hurry. 'I've known him for a long time,' she said, aware the other girl was waiting. 'He's a friend of my mother's. He's writing a history of Legend's Run and their research overlapped. He used to come to the flat—the other one, I mean—quite often,' she added offhandedly and not strictly truthfully, for he hadn't come often at all.

'I see,' Sondra drawled. 'And how have you managed to keep up the acquaintance now your precious mother's off the scene? You can hardly have much in common with a man like Dain. *You're* not doing any research, are you—unless it's research into the advantages to be gained from hanging on to people with money.'

'Believe it or not, I'm not even doing that kind of research,' said Fay, annoyed. 'As a matter of fact, my mother asked Mr Legend to—to keep an eye on me while she's away.' She realised as she said it how it must sound, but she couldn't help that, and she thanked heaven Sondra hadn't turned up in the middle of her encounter with him last night!

'Keep an eye on you!' Sondra exclaimed, half closing her grey-green eyes and looking pained. 'Good lord, what a cheek to ask him to do that! I'm just beginning to realise what a pushy woman your mother is. My father just didn't have a chance ... She wouldn't by any chance be throwing you at Dain's head, would she? *She's* too old for him—I suppose that's why she chose Daddy as her target. But you won't get anywhere with Dain, I can tell you that.'

Fay finished her orange juice and asked innocently, 'Should I want to, Sondra?'

Sondra blinked, momentarily disconcerted, but quickly recovered herself. 'Knowing what inexorable gold-diggers you and your mother are, I'd be surprised if you didn't want to. He's very obviously a good catch. But you'd better know it now—Dain and I are—very close.'

'Are you?' Fay meant to say it indifferently, but she was aware of the note of scepticism in her own voice. If Sondra was implying that Dain Legend was in love with her, Fay wasn't convinced. He was so cynical she couldn't see him falling in love with anyone at all, not even with a girl as attractive and poised as Sondra. As for Sondra's remark that he was a good catch—that might possibly be so financially, but for certain sure, if *she* ever caught him in *her* net, she'd very quickly throw him back in the sea! Though she wasn't going to tell Sondra that.

She made herself a cup of instant coffee and decided to forget about toast. It was getting late, and Sondra's company had taken the edge off her appetite.

'Well, what's in the packet?' Sondra pursued as if she had every right to know, particularly now she had revealed that she and Dain Legend were 'very close'— whatever that might mean. She slid off the stool and found a cup for herself. 'Or is it some deep dark secret?' she asked sarcastically as with a look of distaste she too made herself some instant coffee.

Fay shrugged. 'It's not a secret. He wants me to type something for him, that's all. He told me last night he'd leave it in the service hatch.' She saw the sudden look of fury on Sondra's face and her spine prickled. She should not have mentioned that she had seen Dain last night, of course. As for the typing, though she had almost made up her mind she wasn't going to do it, she wasn't so sure now. At any rate, she wanted to read the manuscript.

'I don't know what to make of you, Fay Douglas,' Sondra gritted through her teeth. 'But I do know that the more I see of you the less I like you. My opinion of you when we first met was that you were a pathetic nonentity, with no looks, no character, and no talents. Now for some reason you seem to think you're really someone.'

Fay's spirits were sinking lower and lower. She had never met anyone before who disliked her so intensely. Even Dain Legend's company was preferable to that of her stepsister, she thought bitterly, as with an effort she forced herself not to strike back. It would only make things worse if the two of them engaged in insults. She drank her coffee without tasting it while Sondra ranted on.

'First you latch on to Tony Thorpe, now it's Dain Legend. What did you do? Invite him down here last night? Or go and present yourself at his flat to make sure he's aware of your existence? However, I'm not making a fuss about Tony, in fact I find your taking him up distinctly amusing. But I warn you, Fay, if you try to worm your way into Dain's life, I shall get really nasty. And I mean *nasty*!'

Fay put down her cup and looked at her without speaking. Inside her head, she said, You're nasty already—and I mean *nasty*!

'For a start,' Sondra went in, 'you won't make excuses for fraternising with him by doing this typing. I don't want you to. There are hundreds of typists in Canberra. Leave that manuscript or whatever it is with me, and I'll hand it over to a competent girl and Dain will be no worse off. In fact it will be to his advantage—and to yours.'

Fay met her eyes. 'I'm sorry, Sondra, I'll make my own arrangements. You seem to forget I'm a working girl. It means money to me.'

Sondra slammed down her half empty cup and reached for the packet of cigarettes at her elbow. She put one in her long holder and lit up with trembling fingers.

'What utter drivel!' she spat. 'With your mother in cheering for you the way she has been you won't need to earn another penny for the rest of your life. You don't need the money, and you'll do as I say and not make excuses!'

Fay very nearly gave in, it was such an ugly conversation. But why should she let Sondra intimidate her? After an instant of indecision she said, 'I'm not making excuses,' then turned away and rinsed her cup at the sink. 'I'll make up my own mind what I do.'

'You'll be sorry!' snapped Sondra. 'I meant what I said.'

Fay grimaced slightly. She picked up the envelope Dain had left for her. 'I'll have to go now. Will you be here tonight, Sondra?'

Sondra didn't answer.

CHAPTER THREE

BECAUSE of her altercation with Sondra, Fay was ten minutes late for work, which displeased Mrs Markham, and it wasn't until her lunchtime that she opened the big envelope Dain Legend had left for her.

She bought some sandwiches and drove down to Regatta Point, and there, sitting in the car eating her lunch, she opened the packet. There was a brief letter attached to the handwritten pages, and she read it quickly.

'Dear Fay, Enclosed is the first half of *Legend's Run*. Please make only a single copy as I expect to do further revision. You shouldn't have a great deal of difficulty deciphering my writing, but pay particular attention to any alterations or marginal notes. If you have any problems, you can telephone me at Legend's Run—at night as I'm rarely at the homestead during the day. I'll trust you to take care of my manuscript as I don't have a copy. I shall be in Canberra in about a week's time and expect the work to be completed by then. I'll pay you by cheque or in cash, whichever you prefer. In the meantime, behave yourself. Yours, Dain Legend.'

Fay grimaced. It was a reasonable enough letter except for that final sentence—'In the meantime, behave yourself'. Oddly, that gave her a sick feeling in the pit of her stomach. Too vividly, she remembered things she had been forcing herself not to remember— his hands so roughly on her shoulders, the button flying off her pyjama jacket. His gritted, 'I could crush you with one hand!'

She turned her mind abruptly to the manuscript and

started reading it. The writing was firm and bold but not, she discovered, all that easy to read, so her progress was slow.

The story started in 1846 when two men arrived from England and bought land in the wild country of New South Wales, on the banks of the Murrumbidgee River. One man was James Legend, the other was his friend William Marshall. That was a coincidence, Fay thought. But Marshall was a common enough name and William Marshall probably bore no relationship at all to Walter and Sondra. In any event, it appeared that after he married, he sold out his share in the property to his partner and bought land elsewhere, though he retained a small dwelling and about twenty acres of ground. The original property from that time became known as Legend's Run—and prospered.

Fay raised her eyes to the lake, though instead of seeing the sparkling blue water with its scattering of sailing boats, she saw Dain Legend—on horseback—riding around among his sheep. It was a role in which she had never actually seen him, of course, and it made her realise how little she knew of him. It was curious to think he was capable of writing this book too—both interestingly and competently. Was she going to do the typing for him? For some reason she was very much tempted to—in spite of Tony's hope that she would spare all the time she could for him, and in spite, too, of Sondra's threat—'Do as I say, or you'll be sorry!'

'I'll toss a coin,' she thought flippantly as she put the sheets back into their envelope. And then it all flew out of her mind as she saw by the clock on the dashboard what time it was. She was going to be late back to work! Mrs Markham wouldn't be pleased—late twice in one day ...

She was quite right. Mrs Markham wasn't pleased, and what she had to say cut Fay to the quick.

'Don't you take your work seriously any more, Fay? You know I have a lot of making up to do today—I can't be in two places at once. Hurry up and get your overall on, for goodness' sake!'

Fay hurried. It was no use making excuses, there weren't any, except that she'd got caught up reading—and thinking about—that damned manuscript.

An hour or so later, when there were so many customers in the shop that Mrs Markham had had to come in and give a hand, Tony appeared. Fay's heart lurched and her face flooded with colour. She caught his eye and smiled and went on attending to the woman she was serving, then dealt with an elderly man who wanted a huge bouquet of roses. Tony wandered round the shop, sniffing at the flowers, and Mrs Markham, who always kept a sharp eye on priorities, presently glided over to see if she could help him.

'I'm just waiting for a word with Fay,' he said with his friendliest smile. Mrs Markham froze. Fay wrapped the roses, and in her hurry gave the gentleman the wrong amount of change, a mistake that Mrs Markham didn't miss. Her cheeks red, Fay hurried guiltily across to Tony and whispered, 'I can only spare a minute, Tony. What did you want?'

'Looks like I've barged in at the wrong time,' he said. 'Sorry about that. I'll cut it short—that old dragon's glowering at me as if I'd come here to set fire to the place! I just felt I couldn't wait till tomorrow, Fay—I wanted to see you. How about tonight?'

'All right,' she said nervously. There was no time to argue, and Mrs Markham had already expressed disapproval of social visits.

'I'll wait for you outside at five-thirty,' Tony told her. 'We'll decide what to do then.'

Fay nodded, and to her further embarrassment he planted a quick kiss on her nose, then grinned cheekily at Mrs Markham before he vanished.

She was taken to task the minute the shop was empty.

'You're slipping, Fay. You've been late twice today. It seems to me despite what you told me the other day you're getting caught up in another world. I've been expecting it, I must admit. Wasn't that the young man who was here with your stepsister?'

'Yes,' Fay admitted helplessly. 'But I'm not getting caught up in another world, Mrs Markham. I'm sorry I was late, but——'

'I'm not interested in a stream of excuses. It's a fact that when you don't really need a job you get careless. And that doesn't suit me. I'm running a business, and I expect you to do what you're paid to do, not to be cutting fifteen minutes off your working day here, and another ten minutes there, as well as spending precious minutes making social arrangements.'

'I'm sorry,' Fay said again. 'But I do want the job——'

'So does the girl I employed while you were away ill. She's been out of work for over two months.'

Fay swallowed. She felt as guilty as if she had taken the job from Judy James. Mrs Markham obviously thought she no longer needed to work. She thought of the free apartment, of the money Walter Marshall had put in the bank for her. If she pleased, she supposed she wouldn't need to work. But she preferred her independence. She didn't want to—to sponge on Walter. No matter what Sondra thought, she was not a gold-digger, and neither was her mother. Though Mrs Markham didn't put it as baldly as Sondra, she evidently believed she was making the most of her luck. It seemed, in fact, that it was going to be an embarrassment to be related by marriage to Walter Marshall, and Fay wished he wasn't quite so wealthy. She'd better do that typing, she reflected. She just might be out of a job...

She felt more cheerful at the end of the day when she was with Tony, their arms linked, his eyes smiling down into hers.

'I've got tickets for a movie,' he told her. 'And I've booked a table for two at the Charcoal restaurant. You don't need to change, do you? You look perfect as you are.'

She laughed at his flattery, but it did her good. She enjoyed the dinner with him, and relaxed over the light-hearted film he had selected. She didn't ask him back to the flat afterwards, because quite possibly Sondra would be there, and she didn't think they'd make a congenial threesome.

As it was, they had coffee and Brandy Alexanders in town, and the conversation got round to Tony's idea of 'whizzing off' to Paris. Fay's lack of enthusiasm must have shown in her face, for suddenly he said with inspiration, 'Look, why don't we both go? You could take three or four weeks off from that job of yours, couldn't you, Fay?'

Fay laughed incredulously. 'You talk as if we lived in England and just had to fly across the Channel!' she exclaimed. 'Paris is half way across the world!'

'What of it? That only makes it all more romantic.'

It did, of course—it certainly did—but Fay wasn't used to thinking so casually of exotic and long-distance holidays. People like Tony and the Marshalls regarded the spending of money differently. For her, the idea of going overseas was a big one. The cost of the air fare was so high, one would want to be away for a long while to get the most out of it.

'Do you have a passport?' Tony wanted to know, leaning across the table and looking into her eyes. Fay nodded, half mesmerised. She and Dodie Hayes had gone mad last year and obtained passports—then discovered they hadn't really saved enough money to take off.

'Well,' said Tony, 'why don't we?'

He had taken her hand in his—her left hand—and was playing with her third finger, ringless, slender. Her mind made a leap and saw a ring on that finger. Dizzily, she saw herself married to the good-looking man opposite her—leaving the job at Hearts and Flowers—leaving the big apartment where Sondra had come to plague her—freed from any further imperious commands and from the intolerable interference of Dain Legend.

'Why don't we go—together?' Tony repeated caressingly. 'Let me get the tickets—tell that old dragon at the flower shop what she can do with her job. We could leave next week——'

Fay laughed excitedly. Her head was spinning, partly from amazement, mostly from the brandy, and she protested weakly, 'But we—we couldn't! And I couldn't possibly let you get the tickets. I—I can pay for myself——'

'Hush,' he ordered, putting a finger against her soft lips. 'Don't talk about money. You think I'm mad, don't you? And so I am.' He leaned forward closer and touched his lips to hers. 'Mad with love for you,' he said softly.

Mad with love for her! Fay heard music playing. Was it really—or was it in her heart? She thought this must be the most romantic, wonderful moment in her life. She knew positively that she was madly in love too, and for the very first time. With Tony—whose eyes were so frank, his hair so golden she longed to touch it. She could hardly breathe. She said laughingly, 'Tony, I—I think I'd better go home. Really I do. I can't think straight. And it's awfully late—I have to get up in the morning.'

'In Paris,' he said softly, 'you can sleep till noon.'

'I wouldn't want to,' she said, still laughing. 'I'd want to be up—to see everything——'

'You will,' he promised. 'You'll see everything. You'll love it. We'll have a heavenly time together. You must come!'

'I don't know,' she said helplessly. 'Honestly, Tony.'

'It's too sudden,' he said with a grin. 'Okay, Fay—sleep on it—dream about it. And tomorrow we'll talk about it again.'

Fay tried to think of her savings. Exactly how much did she have—of her very own? Because she definitely wasn't going to touch Walter's money. She thought wildly of the typing for Dain Legend, and she was sure she must be off her head because she was tempted—unbearably tempted—by Tony's suggestion. Dain Legend, she thought with a little thrill that was far from unpleasant, would be absolutely livid if she took off for Paris with Tony. But—Paris with Tony. Exactly what did it mean?

She said, suddenly cautious, 'Not tomorrow, Tony. I really do have things to do.'

'That typing?' he interrupted with a grimace. 'Well, if you must. But the night after—it will be torture to wait so long, but so long as you tell me yes——'

'I'll see,' she said calmly. It was strange to feel so powerful, to know that her decision mattered so much to him. She felt more adult than she had ever felt before.

It was almost one o'clock in the morning when she got into her car to drive home. She was deadly tired and over-excited, and definitely a tiny bit drunk, and thankful there was so little traffic. At least she had made her decision about the typing now. She would do it and have that little bit extra money that might make all the difference. She could see herself whizzing off across the world with Tony—she could see a ring on her finger, her life changed completely. Goodbye, Mrs Markham, goodbye, Sondra—I don't need your father's money, you see—my husband's manager of the outstation on a big cattle station owned by his father...

She felt ready to fall into bed and to sleep like a log as she went up in the elevator. Everything was marvellous and mixed-up and mad—and she really shouldn't have had that second Brandy Alexander.

The apartment was in darkness and she entered quietly, wondering whether Sondra was there or not. Her bedroom door was shut, but that told her exactly nothing. In her own room, she put the manuscript in its big envelope on her dressing table. Tomorrow night she would make a start on the typing, and she would work like a demon.

When she went into the bathroom to clean her teeth she discovered that Sondra was still around. Her bath oil was there, her toothbrush, the scented soap she used, and a big expensive bottle of body cologne. Fay sighed fatalistically.

Sondra was still asleep when she got up next morning—late again, with shadows under her eyes, and in a panic to get to work on time. Yet did it matter all that much? Wasn't she going for a holiday with Tony—a holiday that would end in——

In the light of day, Fay was not at all sure. She had really been carried away last night, but after all she had known Tony so short a time. She didn't really know what was in his mind, and she could imagine what interpretation Dain Legend would put on the scheme! But she didn't have to tell him a thing about it—and wouldn't. She would play her cards very close to her chest, and before he was aware that anything at all was happening, she would have disappeared. That was, if she decided to go.

Inevitably, she was late for work again.

'I got caught in the traffic,' she told Mrs Markham futilely.

At Hearts and Flowers, life was no longer what it used to be. She and Mrs Markham used to get on quite well together, but now, because her mother had married Walter Marshall, everything had changed. In Mrs Markham's eyes Fay Douglas had become a different person, a girl who no longer cared about her job or business ethics. She could almost feel dismissal in the air. Judy James, who really needed the position, would be reinstalled. *Her* mother hadn't married into money. Mrs Markham, Fay suspected, was just a little jealous, though if she only knew it she didn't need to be.

At lunchtime she found herself hoping Tony would be waiting for her. She badly wanted to reassure herself that it hadn't been just a lot of nonsense he had been talking last night. But instead of Tony, her friend Dodie Hayes was waiting for her—plump, round-eyed, the same ingenuous, goodhearted girl as ever, yet Fay felt it was years since she had seen her, rather than weeks, so much had happened in her own life. But in Dodie's life, nothing had changed, and she was obviously stunned by Fay's altered appearance.

'You look so different,' she commented as they walked to Petrie Place, where they would buy sandwiches and sit eating them near the famous old merry-go-round, as they often did.

'It's only my hair,' said Fay, feeling selfconscious. Yet it wasn't only her hair, she knew perfectly well. It was falling in love—and getting mixed up with Sondra and Dain Legend—and a whole number of things.

'It was rotten luck you didn't get to the wedding,' Dodie sympathised. 'Are you over your 'flu now? I rang the other night, but you must have been out.'

'I probably was,' Fay agreed, and later as they ate

their sandwiches she couldn't resist telling Dodie about Tony. 'I must have been out with Tony Thorpe the night you rang.'

'Who on earth's he?'

'Well, he's a jackeroo,' Fay told her. 'His father owns a cattle station in Queensland, and he's on holiday just now. He knows the Marshalls,' she added, simplifying matters somewhat.

'Are you in love with him?' Dodie asked ingenuously, and Fay blushed.

'A little,' she admitted, and went on laughingly, 'He wants me to go to Paris with him.'

'To Paris!' Dodie positively gaped. 'Just like that? It sounds like a dream—like something out of a movie. I suppose he's awfully rich, like the Marshalls. I never meet people like that. You *are* lucky, Fay. Will you go? And does he want you to—well, to marry him or something?'

Fay finished the sandwich she was eating before she answered. She didn't really know what Tony wanted herself, and she said cautiously, 'He hasn't asked me— yet. But I guess it could happen. We just sort of—fell for each other the minute we met. He only suggested we should go to Paris last night, and nothing's really been decided. I still feel dizzy when I think of it.'

'I should say so!' Dodie agreed. 'I'd love to meet him. Is he good-looking? And how old?'

'About twenty-five or six, I suppose,' said Fay, then went on to describe him, thinking as she did so that he must sound totally unreal.

'If he's as terrific as you make him sound,' Dodie commented when she'd finished, 'then I guess you will go to Paris. It doesn't look as if you and I will ever take that trip to Europe anyhow, does it? At the rate I'm going I'll never have enough money. Maybe I should get a new hair-style,' she added with a grin. 'But where on earth would I meet a man like that? I don't know people like the Marshalls. Anyhow, how are you getting on with that man your mother asked to look after you—Dain Legend? One of the girls in the office knows him—or at least, she knows all about him. She says he has a terrible reputation with women. You should watch out, Fay.'

Fay made a face. 'Don't worry, he's not interested in me that way. He detests me, in fact. And I can't stand him either.' She changed the subject to talk about the film she had seen with Tony, and before they went back to work they agreed they must meet and go to a movie one night, and have another natter, as Dodie put it. 'If I can rake up a decent male, we could make it a foursome,' she remarked. 'I'm really dying to meet Tony Thorpe!'

Fay was back to work three minutes early, and Mrs Markham had no cause for complaint. That evening she drove back home with the firm intention of making a start on that typing for the hateful Dain Legend. Sondra wasn't going to frighten her off it, she needed the extra money to go away with Tony. She couldn't let him pay her fare—not unless he wanted her to marry him, of course, that would be different. Suppose he asked her, she wondered, would she say yes? She wasn't sure. She knew Dain Legend wouldn't approve, and to be honest she knew her mother would think her foolishly hasty too.

Sondra was out, as she had more or less expected. She couldn't imagine Sondra spending an evening at home—cooking a meal for herself, even washing her hair. Sondra's hair would always be shampooed at the hairdressers. Then she found her things gone from the bathroom, her bedroom emptied of her personal belongings. So she had moved out again—till next time. Well, that was great.

Fay had a quick meal—a tomato and cheese omelette—then went to her room to fetch the manuscript. It simply wasn't there—and she could have sworn she had left it, still in the envelope, on top of her dressing table. Fay stared dismayed, then hunted feverishly—first in her room, then through the rest of the house. But without success. The manuscript was nowhere to be found, nor was the letter. 'I'll trust you to look after it,' Dain had written. 'I don't have a copy.' And Sondra had said, 'You're not to type for him. I don't want you to.' Had she taken it? Fay could think of no other way it could have disappeared, and she couldn't help thinking it quite possible that Sondra had read the letter and planned for Dain to get the impression that Fay was simply not to be trusted. How mean and malicious! Fay wished she hadn't been so careless as to leave it in the flat with her, but she just wasn't used to thinking of people that way. It had never occurred to her that Sondra could be 'nasty' in that particular fashion.

Well, she would have to get it back somehow, but she didn't really know what to do. All she could think of was to telephone Sondra in her father's house in Queanbeyan and ask her straight out if she had the manuscript. And take it from there.

When she rang Queanbeyan it was to discover that Sondra wasn't there.

'This is the housekeeper, Mrs Turner. Who is that calling?'

'It's Fay Douglas, Mrs Turner.'

'Oh—Miss Douglas. Miss Marshall called in today for some clothes and then she went on to the country cottage. She's going to spend a few days working on her pottery.'

Fay listened mystified. She hadn't known Sondra did pottery, nor did she know where the country cottage was, but she kept her ignorance to herself.

'Would you give me her telephone number, please? I want to get in touch with her rather urgently.'

'She doesn't have the telephone, Miss Douglas. I suggest you call Legend's Run if it's important. Mr Legend will make sure she gets the message.' She gave Fay the Legend's Run number, and Fay thanked her and hung up thoughtfully, feeling vaguely put out. So Sondra's cottage was in the vicinity of Legend's Run! It occurred to her that perhaps the William Marshall of Dain's history was related to the Walter Marshalls after all. Perhaps Sondra's 'country cottage' was the small dwelling the Marshalls had retained, in its twenty acres of ground.

She had a definite feeling of being at a disadvantage as she picked up the telephone again and dialled the number Mrs Turner had given her.

It was Dain who answered, and she was immediately filled with nervousness.

'Is that you, Mr Legend?' she asked quite unnecessarily.

'Yes. It's Fay, is it? What do you want? Are you in some sort of trouble?'

'No, of course not,' she denied at once. 'I was trying to get in touch with Sondra.'

There was a slight pause, then he said definitely, 'Well, she's not here. And if she's at the cottage, she's probably up to her ears in clay. What's so important?'

'Nothing really,' she said, quailing at the thought of telling him about his precious manuscript and finding she simply couldn't do it. 'I—I just wondered if she'd managed to—to pass on that typing before she left Canberra today.'

'What the hell are you talking about?' he exclaimed explosively. '*You're* doing that typing—it's designed to keep you out of mischief. Do you mean to tell me you've handed it over to Sondra?' Her spine prickled at his tone. He sounded as if it were a crime! Well, she hadn't handed it over, but she couldn't say so now. Instead she told him rapidly, 'I mightn't be able to do it. I'm—I'm thinking of taking a holiday—going away.'

'Going away? Where the devil to? And who are you going with?'

Fay hesitated. She didn't have the courage to tell him that, either, and anyhow, she hadn't made up her mind yet. She said evasively, 'I thought my mother would have told you that Dodie Hayes and I were—were planning a trip overseas.'

'Maybe she did,' he said when she paused. 'But not that you'd be taking off in the near future. At all events, you're not to do a thing without discussing it with me first. Meanwhile, you can do that typing. I'll see Sondra and you can expect my manuscript back in your hands tomorrow. Is that clear?'

'Yes, but——' she began to protest, but he slammed the receiver down in her ear and she sat looking blankly into space.

Now what had she done? Sondra would think she'd told tales, and Dain Legend—did he mean he'd be handing over the manuscript tomorrow? She should never have breathed a word about going away, told that half lie about herself and Dodie. She wished she had never touched the phone. And she wouldn't have, if Sondra hadn't pinched the manuscript. It was a vicious circle, and her life was getting into more and more of a complicated mess.

Wretchedly, she decided to wash her hair.

The next day, just before noon, Dain Legend came into the shop and without even glancing in Fay's direction went straight to Mrs Markham. Fay felt herself flush scarlet and then grow pale. Mrs Markham was going to be furious. She didn't hear what either of them said, but a minute later Mrs Markham came over to her and said icily, 'You'd better take your lunch hour now, Fay, since your—guardian's come to town especially to see you.' In a lower tone she added, 'But I warn you, I've made up my mind. I'll ask Judy James to come back. You're going from bad to worse—you don't care any more. Your head's full of personal matters these days.'

Fay looked at her helplessly. Was it her fault that Dain Legend had come barging in here, demanding she take her lunch hour immediately? It wasn't even as if she wanted to. In fact, she was dreading what he would have to say to her, and the questions he would ask. She went to the cloakroom and got out of her overall, stared at her face in the small wall mirror and tried to smooth out the little frown between her brows. She was wearing a white skirt and a dark brown sleeveless blouse and she didn't look too bad. She had planned to do some shopping in her lunch hour, actually—for dinner in the flat with Tony. She hadn't yet decided what she would tell him about the holiday in Paris. She wanted to get a few things clear first, most of all just what it all meant to him, and if he were serious about her.

Feeling more than slightly flustered, she went back through the shop. She could see Dain Legend waiting for her outside, and Mrs Markham was staring through the window at him. She turned to Fay and asked bluntly, '*Is* that your guardian, Fay? Or is this just another—friendship you've struck up on the basis of your elevated position in life? That man's too old for you, you know—too worldly.'

'Mr Legend doesn't tell untruths,' she said, knowing she sounded defensive. 'My mother asked him to be my guardian while she's away. I'm sorry he wants me to go to lunch now, but it's not my fault, and I don't really want to go. I have some shopping to do, and now I shan't have time for it.'

Mrs Markham looked at her thoughtfully. 'I don't know what to think of you lately, Fay. Up till now we've managed very well together, though I won't pretend you've been anything like perfect, but these days you're not the same girl at all, and I can't say the change is for the better. This business now—does it occur to you it's upset *my* plans? Or can you only think of your own shopping?'

'I'm sorry,' Fay said futilely, and after a moment left the shop, her eyes downcast.

Dain had little to say when she joined him. He took her to a hotel restaurant, very smart and very expensive, and ordered a meal without bothering to consult her taste. Two tomato juices—no wine. Rainbow trout and salad. It was a simple meal and it suited Fay, though she wondered if a glass of wine would have steadied her jittery nerves. It might, of course, have had the opposite effect. She'd forgotten what a forceful-looking man he was, so dark and powerful, and again she saw the cruelty in the line of his sensual mouth. He wore a light-coloured suit with a striped shirt and a plain dark red tie, and he looked very much the city man except for the deep bronze of his skin. When he looked across the table and found her staring at him she turned slightly to glance through the window into the wide tree-lined street, aware of the almost frantic beating of her heart. She had a feeling she wasn't going to enjoy her lunch.

Leaning towards her, he said in a low voice, 'You're quite intent on making yourself a nuisance, aren't you, Fay Douglas? Like some irresponsible school kid playing up on the new maths master.'

She moistened her upper lip with the tip of her tongue.

'Why do you say that?'

'Because it's an unpleasant fact. I very nearly changed my mind and didn't come in today. I had a strong inclination to wash my hands of you altogether. However, there are one or two things I suppose we must talk about.' He sat back as the waitress placed their meal on the table, then, taking up his knife and fork, said abruptly, 'First of all, the matter of my manuscript.'

Fay crimsoned. 'I—didn't you see Sondra?'

'Yes, I saw Sondra. She hasn't got it. So what exactly was the point in lying to me?' He took a mouthful of his food and looked at her, his eyes dark and angry.

Fay reached for her tomato juice. She thought food would choke her. Sondra must have the manuscript, there was no other way it could have vanished. But of course she'd denied it, and of course she was showing Fay how nasty she could be. Fay would obviously have to be insane to try anything on with Dain Legend! But now what was she to say? 'Sondra's lying.' How would that sound? She set her glass down and for a moment watched him eating his fish.

'I—I didn't mean Sondra *had* it,' she said at last, groping for words. 'But she offered—said—she could find someone to do the typing if I didn't want— couldn't manage it.'

He smiled unpleasantly and studied her face in a way that made her shrink inwardly.

'Suppose you stop trying to wriggle out of the idiotic lies you told me. Sondra didn't even know you had my manuscript until I mentioned it to her. She suggested you might have—mislaid it, and were trying for some reason to put the blame on her. She apparently has a feeling you don't like her much ... Have you lost it, Fay?'

Fay's face was dead white. It was a mean and miserable thing Sondra was doing and her blood boiled—not only on her own behalf but, curiously enough, on Dain's. She could imagine how her mother would feel if something happened to one of her manuscripts. All that work, irretrievably lost. After a second she looked him straight in the eye and said definitely, 'No, Mr Legend, I have not lost your manuscript.' As she spoke, she promised herself that she would get it back somehow, no matter what.

He looked back at her levelly.

'Very well, I'll accept that as the truth. And that being so, you can get on with the work and forget about passing it over to some other typist. Remember I want it by next week ... Aren't you going to eat your lunch? For God's sake don't sit there staring at me as if you'd lost your senses. You're not sick, are you?'

'I'm just not very hungry,' she said, and forced herself to pick up a morsel of the fish on her fork and put it in her mouth.

'One other thing,' he remarked, watching her aloofly. 'This sudden idea of yours to go off on a holiday overseas. Frankly I'd be delighted if you were to disappear completely. I have enough on my plate at the moment without the added complication of a stupid girl making a constant nuisance of herself. Unfortunately, I'm responsible for you whether I like it or not, and I want full details of your plans. I'll then give them my consideration—and quite likely put a stop to them. I won't know what you're up to on the other side of the world.'

Fay almost choked on her food.

'You're not going to have full details! In fact, I refuse to discuss my affairs with you.'

'Now that's very interesting,' he drawled. 'I wonder what you've got to hide? Are you and your girl friend not going away alone? Or are you just a pair of birdbrains racing off to launch yourselves into every kind of adventure you can find?'

'Don't be ridiculous,' Fay broke in, her cheeks hot. 'Dodie's not that kind of girl and neither am I. Anyhow, I'll do as I please. I don't have to tell you anything.'

He studied her from under lowered brows. He had finished his meal and it was clear Fay had lost interest in hers, and he indicated to the waitress that they would have coffee. Fay looked at her watch nervously.

'I have to go back to work soon.'

'When I've finished with you,' he said relentlessly.

'No,' she retorted, suddenly determined. 'You're not going to keep me late. You won't get a thing out of me—and besides, I—I have some shopping to do.'

'Sit down,' he ordered as she began to rise. His voice was so sharp, so savage, that involuntarily she obeyed.

'Are you planning to go overseas?' he demanded.

'Why not?'

'With this girl Dodie—whatever her name is?'

Her eyes fell before his.

'Didn't I say so?' she prevaricated. 'And anyhow, does it matter who I go with?'

'Yes, it does,' he said explosively. Neither of them had noticed that the coffee had come, but now Fay found herself reaching for her cup as if for a lifeline. Anything that would give her something to do and save her from Dain Legend's merciless gaze.

'I no longer believe a word you say,' he remarked presently. 'I'm staying in town tonight. When you've finished your evening meal you can come upstairs to my apartment and we'll finish our talk.'

'I'm having a guest tonight,' she flung at him. It had stung to have him say he didn't believe a word she said, but the trouble was, he was beginning to be right. She had been more or less lying, and she detested lies. She wasn't going to tell any more.

'Who's your guest?'

'Tony Thorpe,' she said at once, and swallowed down some of the hot coffee.

'I told you not to invite him to your flat.'

'I don't do everything you tell me!'

'I'm aware of that ... Well, you can expect a second guest at about eight-thirty.'

'I don't think I will,' she said defiantly. It would be unbearable to have him turn up when Tony was there—ask questions, make himself unpleasant and officious as if she were a child who was misbehaving. She needed to talk to Tony privately anyhow, so she could make up her mind about Paris. Maddeningly, she could feel herself weakening already, and that was Dain Legend's fault, she thought rebelliously.

'I'll be there,' he said, 'so don't say you haven't been warned.'

'You're hateful and I loathe you!' she burst out. She got up from her chair and this time he didn't stop her. She didn't say thank you for the lunch, and he didn't say, I'll see you tonight. At all events, she knew what she was going to do.

She hurried to the hotel foyer and found a telephone, then rang through to the motel where Tony was staying. He wasn't there, so she left a message for him asking him to meet her outside Hearts and Flowers at five-forty-five. They'd eat in town.

Then she hurried back to work. She didn't need to do any shopping now.

'I'm sorry about this,' she told Tony when they met. They had found a place to eat, and Tony had ordered pre-dinner drinks—a sherry for her, a Martini for himself. 'I just found I couldn't ask you to the flat after all.'

'Don't worry!' he said. 'So long as we spend the evening together.' He raised his glass and looked at her over it. 'I've got a confession to make, Fay.'

'What?'

'I've booked those flights to Paris.'

She stared at him speechlessly, completely taken aback. 'But—but I——' she finally stuttered, but he interrupted her.

'Now you can't say no. And won't it be a lot more fun than messing about in Canberra? Sure it'll cost money—but what's money for after all but to enjoy, to have fun? We owe it to ourselves to celebrate our meeting by doing something really crazy—something we'll never forget. Don't you agree?'

Fay was still looking at him helplessly and he leaned towards her across the table. 'Fay, what's the matter? The other night you were all set to go, now you've come over all cautious. Why? Don't you trust me? Don't you feel the way I do?'

Fay looked at him through her lashes, stunned anew by his good looks, his blue eyes that were so clear and candid. Of course she trusted him—anyone would trust a man so honest-looking—and she was well aware she was more than a little in love with him. It was just that—well, it wasn't the sort of thing she was used to doing. It was—crazy, and she'd always been so sensible.

'Of course I trust you, Tony,' she said slowly. 'Why wouldn't I?'

He shrugged and put his hand over hers. 'You never know. Someone could be trying to mess things up for us. Your mother's friend Dain Legend, for instance. Have you told him our plans?'

'Of course not! It's nothing to do with him.'

'That's right,' Tony agreed. 'It's nothing to do with anyone in the world but you and me. A love affair's a very private thing.'

That was true, Fay thought.

After that they had dinner, and Tony ordered a bottle of wine. And by the time they had finished eating, and finished the wine, Fay knew that of course she would go to Paris with him. She'd be mad not to. It was the kind of way-out, romantic thing people did when they had fallen in love.

Later he took her to a disco and the music throbbed through her blood and she had the giddy feeling that she had never lived before. This was life—and she was as madly in love with Tony as he was with her.

Walking to the car park afterwards Tony said, 'There's one rather sordid little detail, Fay—I may have to borrow some money from you on Monday, for our return tickets. I've wired to Queensland for the money, but the sooner we fix it all up at the travel agents the better. In fact, if we don't confirm the booking by full payment, we may miss out. It's not as if we were arranging things months in advance. I thought two weeks from today would give us adequate time. You'll be able to give a week's notice to that old dragon you work for and then we can have a few days in Sydney at one of the big hotels. How does that sound?'

'Lovely,' Fay murmured dizzily, sure she must be dreaming.

When they reached her car he kissed her goodnight. 'I'll see you tomorrow, Fay. You're free Saturday afternoons, aren't you? And then we can have all Sunday together. And on Monday—if you wouldn't mind arranging about that loan, just for a couple of days——'

'Of course, Tony,' she agreed willingly. 'But I'm going to pay my own fare, you know.'

'We'll see about that,' he said teasingly, and kissed her again before she slid into the car.

She drove back home in something of a daze. She was going to have her trip overseas—she really was! Oh, it wasn't going to be as she'd planned. She and Dodie had talked about flying to London and from there doing some tours—north to Scotland, across the Channel to Europe. As it was, it was just to be Paris, romantic Paris, and with Tony Thorpe. It was unreal! What on earth would her mother think? The fact was, as Mrs Markham had said, Fay Douglas had changed. She was doing things she would never have dreamed of doing before. She was sure she could explain it all to Claire, and that her mother would believe her. Dain Legend was different. She could never explain to him; he had the wrong sort of mind. So she just wouldn't tell him a thing—when he finally caught up with her. She'd certainly won a victory over him by staying out tonight!

As she got into the elevator in the apartment block, she remembered his manuscript again and felt a pang of guilt. She really felt bad about that, and her head began to ache. Oh dear, instead of going out with Tony tonight she should have driven over towards Bungendore and found Sondra's 'country cottage' and—and attacked her about the matter. Surely once she had convinced her she wasn't in the least interested in Dain Legend Sondra would hand the thing over. And then—then she could get the typing done before she and Tony went to Sydney.

Suddenly her mind was seething with all the things she would have to do—the typing, telling Mrs Markham she was leaving, fixing up what clothes she would take. It would be winter in the northern hemisphere, she suddenly realised. She would need warm things—maybe she would do some shopping in Sydney——

The lift stopped, the doors opened, and still deep in her thoughts she walked along the corridor towards her front door, groping in her handbag for her key as she did so. Then, as if it were a nightmare, she just couldn't get the key into the lock. She went cold all over. Where on earth was she? This wasn't her flat—— Flustered, she clumsily dropped the key and as she stooped to pick it up the door opened. She straightened up, an apology freezing on her lips as she discovered Dain Legend glowering down at her.

CHAPTER FOUR

FAY stood as if petrified. He wore closely fitting black pants and that was all. Nothing on his feet, and his chest—it was somehow shockingly bare. She tore her eyes away from the dark hair on it and raised them to his face. He had a cigarette between his lips and his black brows were drawn.

'I'm—I'm sorry. I must have come up to the wrong floor,' she began to stammer, when a muscular, deeply tanned arm shot out and she was caught in an inescapable grip.

'I've been looking for you, Fay Douglas,' he gritted. 'Where the hell have you been?'

'Out,' she heard herself say defiantly, though a shock went through her when she saw the expression on his face. He dragged her helpless into his apartment and she heard the door shut firmly behind her. It was useless to gasp that she wasn't coming in—that it was late—that she was going to bed. Dain wasn't impressed.

'God knows whether you came scratching at my door by accident or design,' he said, his nostrils dilating. 'But now you're here you'll damned well come in. I have things to say to you.'

They were in his sitting room by now and he thrust her on to a couch—black leather and sinfully comfortable and squashy, she found as she sank into it. The room was sombre and very masculine, decorated in brown and black relieved by touches of ivory. There was a solid, low coffee table that looked as if it had been hewn out of bush timber a long time ago, its surface glossy, its corners rounded with use. The carpet was dark brown and on one wall, giving the whole room a lift, was an enormous painting—a primitive, and rather Rousseau-like, Fay thought dimly. In it, a maiden in white crouched in a jungle of huge leaves, through which prowled an animal with golden eyes. Fay felt like the maiden, and Dain was the beast, and though his eyes were black they were no less terrifying, no less savage.

'Brace yourself,' she heard him say, 'because I'm not listening to any more lies and prevarications from you. We're going to have every card on the table. Do you need a brandy to give you strength, or will you wait till I've finished with you?'

Fay had had quite enough alcohol for one night, and she tried to draw a deep breath to steady herself, but found it was impossible. All she could do was shake her head and try to control her shivering. Dain talked about the dangers of entertaining men in her apartment, but never in her life had she felt more in danger than she did right now, with this fearsome, bare-chested man sitting so near her and holding her captive.

'Now we'll hear all about your holiday plans,' he said harshly. 'Full details and no omissions.'

Fay said nothing. She clasped her hands tightly and wished she didn't feel so tired—that her head wasn't aching—that she hadn't drunk so much wine or danced so long in the disco.

'So you're not going with your girl friend,' he pronounced after a long silence. 'It's Tony Thorpe, isn't it?'

Still she didn't answer, but her cheeks crimsoned and he went on remorselessly, 'The minute your mother's out of sight you're kicking up your heels and losing your head over the first man who comes along. How far has it gone? Have you slept with him yet?'

Fay sat up straight, her cornflower-blue eyes angry. 'I wish you'd mind your own business! It's not like that at all. And anyhow, I'm not a child—I'm nearly twenty and I'll do as I please!'

'So you keep telling me,' he said coldly. He looked as if he would like to shake her. 'What you don't seem to realise is that you may regret it for the rest of your life. As for your being nearly twenty, you're more like sixteen from what I've seen of you—and that's probably your mother's fault. Charming she might be and no doubt she loves you, but while she's been chasing her career along, you seem to have been detained in childhood—and now you've been left on your own with not a scrap of sense or of worldly experience to draw on.'

'And of course, you have loads of both,' Fay retorted, remembering what Dodie had said about his reputation with women. 'Especially the—worldly experience.'

Heavens, now he was going to shake her! She shrank back involuntarily, but he was only reaching for another cigarette. She watched him light up and thought, he's full of nerves, smoking so much.

He looked at her narrow-eyed as he put the cigarette between his lips and drew on it. 'All right,' he said, his voice dead level, 'so I've had plenty of experience. But I'll remind you I'm roughly fifteen years older than you are.'

'Are you? All the same, I'll have to hurry to catch up, even in fifteen years, won't I?' she said smartly, recovering somewhat now that the shaking had not eventuated.

His glance moved over her slowly, and she had the feeling he was counting ten so as not to lose his temper, and when he spoke again it was to ask sharply, 'I'm right, aren't I? You're planning this—holiday with Tony Thorpe.'

'What if I am?' she said defiantly. She hadn't meant to admit to anything actually, but he'd guessed, and she suddenly felt she didn't care. She had nothing to hide, after all. She knew what Tony was like, she trusted him.

'You're a fool if you let yourself be talked into it, Fay, and it seems as if I'll have to be brutally frank and tell you why. Irresistibly attractive though you, and no doubt a good many other girls, find him, he's an adventurer—a fortune-hunter. What he's interested in right now is jingling some of the Marshall money in his pockets. Sondra knows all about it, he hung around her a year ago, but she worked it all out for herself and didn't get her fingers burned. You're not sharp enough for that—you're easy prey. Think it over for a minute, Fay.'

He leaned towards her and looked hard at her from under his dark brows, and she felt her heart pounding. This was the craziest thing she'd ever heard! She had nothing to do with the Marshalls' money. She was a working girl—Tony knew that. Besides, he didn't need other people's money. She knew his background. She said heatedly, 'Walter Marshall's bank account has nothing to do with me nor I with it, Mr Legend. I'm—I'm a working girl, and I'm independent.'

Dain drew on his cigarette and smiled crookedly. 'Is that so? You're paying the rent for the flat downstairs, are you? If so, then you must be the highest paid shopgirl around Canberra.'

Fay bit her lip. 'All right, I'm not paying the rent,' she admitted stiffly. 'But I'm—I'm looking after the place. And anyhow, you're just splitting hairs.'

He shrugged his broad shoulders and ashed his cigarette in an enormous silver ashtray on the floor, then looked at her sardonically. 'But you're all ready to shoot off overseas at a moment's notice, aren't you? So much for your caretaking value!'

Fay felt enraged. She glanced at him through her lashes to see if he was looking pleased with himself, but he was frowning, the smoke from his cigarette curling up from the hand that rested on his knee. Suddenly he tossed it down in the ashtray and looked at her fully.

'Are you in love with Tony Thorpe?'

Fay blinked. What a fool she was to sit here and let him question her like this! If she'd refused right from the start to say anything at all, then he might have given up. As it was, he went on and on. 'Is there any reason why I shouldn't be?' she asked, and tried to look bored.

'I thought I'd just given you a reason,' he said, his sensual mouth twisting in a smile that wasn't amused. 'Though God knows, if you're so infatuated that you can't see anything beyond it, then you're well and truly tied to the mast and I guess I can't help you.'

'I didn't ask you to help me,' she retorted.

'I'm aware of that. But unfortunately I promised your mother I'd be around if anything should go wrong.'

'Well, nothing has gone wrong. So you can mind your own business and let me and Tony mind ours. And if you knew anything at all, you'd know that Tony's father owns a big cattle station up in Queensland,' she finished triumphantly.

'And how much do you know about it?' he said sceptically, his eyes rock hard and completely devoid of sympathy. 'Only what he's told you.'

'Oh, you—you're the type of man who doesn't believe anyone or anything,' she stammered.

He shrugged. 'Is your boy-friend throwing the party—paying all your expenses—and with no strings attached?'

'I don't expect him to. I'm paying my own expenses,' she said, flushing.

Dain raised one eyebrow. 'Walter—made you a generous present before he went away, I believe.'

Fay could guess who had told him that—and hated

the thought that he had discussed her with Sondra. She said fiercely, 'I don't see it as a present. It's a—a trust—for emergencies. I won't be touching it. I do have something of my own, even if I am only a shopgirl.'

Dain slanted her a look. 'Did I say that?'

'You implied it.'

He grunted and got up from the couch. 'What do you want? If I suggest you have any kind of a pipeline to the Marshall coffers you don't like it. Nor do you like being designated as a struggling shopgirl. It seems I have to grapple with female sensitivity along with everything else.'

'From what I've heard of you, you should be used to—to everything female,' Fay flung at him unwisely. 'I'm certainly glad I'm not one of your women, anyway!'

'I'm inclined to praise God for the same thing,' he said tersely. 'But you'll be one of Tony Thorpe's women if you go away with him, nothing's surer ... Do you object if I get myself a Scotch?'

'You can do what you like,' she said angrily.

He turned his back, and as he crossed the room to the bar, she got up from the couch and walked swiftly and silently towards the door.

'I'm going now. Goodnight.'

She spoke too soon, because the next moment Dain caught her round the waist from behind, his hands hard and cruel on her hipbones.

'You're not going yet,' he said in her ear. 'I haven't finished with you, and I know just how you're feeling.'

'How am I feeling?' she asked, her heart thudding, too conscious of the warmth and pressure of his fingers, and too afraid to struggle for fear of what would happen next.

'Full of hatred,' he said. 'You've never liked me, and now I've made you uneasy, haven't I?' His hands were

hard no longer, instead they were almost caressing—
gentle, persuasive.

'I'm not—uneasy,' she breathed. 'I just—just——'

'Then you damned well should be,' he said softly.
'You should be hellishly uneasy. You should be wondering if I'm right about Tony Thorpe—however much
you hate me for saying what I have.'

He spoke against her hair and the warmth of his
breath sent a tremor along her nerves. If she hadn't
been uneasy before, she was now, though not for the
reason Dain meant.

'You should be looking to see if there aren't a few
visible cracks in your rosy image of your handsome
boy-friend,' said Dain. He moved one hand to her
diaphragm and she drew a sharp breath. '*Think*, Fay.
How much do you really know about the guy? Hate me
all you like for saying it, but the fact is that when it
comes to attracting a man, money can be a much bigger
draw than a pretty face.'

'Well, I don't have either,' Fay said huskily, and
twisted rapidly out of his grasp. He caught her by the
shoulders and swung her round to face him, holding her
helpless and looking compellingly into her eyes.

'Come on now,' he said. 'You're certainly not without physical charm. As for money—knowing Walter,
I'd say you could ask what you liked of him, and get it.
He's a very generous man, and I have no doubt he's
kindly disposed towards his attractive wife's young
daughter.'

'I—I wish you'd shut up,' Fay muttered under her
breath. She had a mad impulse to do something violent—to—to smack his face, hard. Her hand moved and
he caught her wrist and twisted it.

'Just—don't, Fay.'

'Don't what?'

'Don't run off into the blue distance with your

would-be lover. Wait. Work it out here, in Canberra.'

'Under your eye? So you can interfere and—and spoil everything?' Fay was quivering and very much aware of his strength. She had never been in a situation like this before—threatened by a man's superior muscular strength—and deep down she was frightened. 'Let me go! You're hurting my wrist.'

He took no notice at all. 'Does he talk about marrying you?' he demanded roughly. 'Or are you just going to have a good time together in Europe?'

'Oh, leave me alone!' Tears had flown to her eyes. 'It's all perfectly simple. I've—I've always wanted to go to Europe and Dodie can't make it yet. So why shouldn't I go with Tony? It's much safer with a man, anyhow,' she finished with a rush.

'Is it? How do you work that out?' Dain's black eyes burned down at her, and in them and on the curve of his wide mouth she saw a cruel cynicism. 'Are you really as ingenuous as you look, Fay? Do you feel safe here—with me—now? The way we are——' As he said the words he drew her forcefully towards him until her body was crushed helplessly against his, and she could feel the heat of his bare torso intimately through her thin blouse. His lips found hers inexorably and he was kissing the life out of her, while his body moulded itself closer and closer to hers, until she was aware of him with every part of her. Her heart pounded, her pulses raced as she submitted helplessly, and though she was frightened to death of the way he was kissing her— deeply, exploringly—her senses were responding crazily.

She was dizzy and almost swooning when he let her go.

'That's how safe you are with a man,' he told her. 'I could rape you here and now if I wanted.' He was breathing hard and he spoke harshly. 'Had you thought about that kind of thing? Or is sex a price you'd willingly pay for some other kind of protection?'

Fay couldn't speak. Her eyes were fixed on his bare chest, and she watched it rise and fall rhythmically. She wanted to run away, but her legs had turned to jelly, and she leaned against the wall instead, swallowing and swallowing, her mouth trembling.

'Well?' demanded Dain, and she shifted her gaze to his face with an effort. His eyes glittered down at her mockingly and she hated him. She knew he found her lack of sophistication amusing and she longed to find something hurtful to say. But what could she ever say that would hurt so hard a man? She mattered nothing to him. All he wanted was to crush her—to force her to obey his commands.

She saw the corner of his lip curve. 'That's reduced you to silence, hasn't it, Fay Douglas? I guess no man has kissed you that way before. But you can expect a lot more than mere kissing if you deliberately expose yourself to danger. I hope it will persuade you to do some in-depth thinking, at all events—before you pack your bags and fly off with someone you scarcely know.'

Fay found breath enough to say, 'Tony's—not—like you.'

He sent her a contemptuous look through half-closed eyes. 'If he's a male, he is. Your attractions are not inconsiderable, you know ... Can you find your way down to your own flat now?'

Fay said nothing. Somehow she reached the door and the minute he opened it she stepped through and didn't answer his goodnight. The elevator was there, and she got into it without looking back, because she hadn't heard the door close. Then as the lift descended, she leaned back weakly against the wall. 'Pig! Beast!' she said aloud in a voice that had a distinct tremor in it. No wonder his wife had left him—whether she was unfaithful to him or not. She had a strong suspicion that her mother had been wrong about his marriage. If Dain's wife had left it was probably because he was unfaithful to her. She would certainly never tolerate a man like that—domineering, know-it-all, never hesitating to use his brute strength to subdue—living by the assumption that might is right. All the same, he wasn't going to win this battle against her. She'd show him he couldn't poison *her* mind with his cynicism and his lack of faith in other people.

Back in the seclusion of her own apartment, and thankful that Sondra wasn't there, she went to her bedroom. She put a hand to her mouth, feeling it bruised and swollen from the assault of Dain's kiss as he had forced her lips apart and—— Oh God, she couldn't think about it! She could still feel the pressure of his body against her own—his heat, his hard muscles, his unfamiliar masculinity...

Breathing fast, she got out of her clothes and ran naked down the hall to the bathroom. As she turned on the shower she saw her reflection in the wall mirror—her white body, her pale face with a red spot burning high on each cheekbone. Her mouth was trembling and it looked swollen. He was—he was a brute of a man! Her mother—Walter—they'd both of them just about have a heart attack if they knew how her 'protector' had been behaving. Protector! He was more of an *aggressor*! And he had the cheek to warn her against a decent man like Tony, she thought as she stepped under the warm water. As for all those things he had said about Tony, she didn't believe a word of them. He just had a cynical, suspicious mind.

'I never want to see him again,' she decided later as she draped her bathtowel around her and went back to her bedroom, there to remember, with a sinking heart, Dain's manuscript. However much she hated him, she had to get that back.

Sondra rang in the morning just as Fay was about to leave for work. Fay was looking terrible. She had scarcely slept and when she had, it had been to dream that that man was kissing her again, so that she woke sobbing, as if unable to escape from his embrace.

'Fay?' Sondra's voice said. 'Did you see Dain yesterday?'

Fay almost choked. Had she seen Dain! 'Yes, I—I had lunch with him,' she said.

'What lies did you tell him about his book?' Sondra demanded.

'I told him I hadn't lost it,' Fay said wearily. 'I know you have it, Sondra, and I'll be grateful if you'll let me have it back right away.'

'I might do that,' Sondra drawled. 'It will depend on how co-operative you decide to be. If you're going to be difficult, then I just might destroy the thing.'

'You wouldn't!' Fay gasped. 'You must know all the work that's been put into it. And you know—you've read my letter—you know Dain—Mr Legend—doesn't have a copy——'

'Then it's all in your hands, isn't it?' said Sondra. 'I want a promise from you that you'll keep out of Dain's way—*right* out of his way. No more lunching with him or seeing him in the apartment.'

Fay glanced at her watch anxiously. If she didn't get this conversation finished she would be late for work. She said quickly, 'You don't have to worry about my relationship with Mr Legend, Sondra. He doesn't like me any more than I like him. I can't help it if you don't believe me—it just happens to be true. And if you're reasonable you'll see it's very difficult to say I won't see him at all. He promised my mother——'

Sondra cut her short. 'I don't want to hear all that rigmarole again. Now listen—I'm in my father's house in Queanbeyan at the moment, but I'll be going back to the cottage later on. It's on the Bungendore Road and not hard to find. You can come and see me there this afternoon.' She explained how to get there, while Fay listened nervously. 'Is that clear?'

'Yes,' Fay said hurriedly, 'I'll be there. I must go now—Goodbye.' She hung up, then snatched up her handbag and the car keys and practically ran from the flat.

Of course she arrived late at the shop. It seemed to happen more often than not these days, and Mrs Markham drew her own conclusions, after taking in her shadowed eyes and general nerviness.

'I suppose you've been out till all hours of the night with some of your rich young friends,' she commented. 'You don't look capable of doing even half a day's work with any kind of reliability. I'll give you just one more chance, Fay, and after that you can leave.'

Fay didn't protest, though her heart sank. She hated the thought of getting the sack, even though she would have to give up her job if she went away with Tony. Though in that case, it might only be temporary.

As the morning went by, she realised Mrs Markham was right; she was far from efficient. She was clumsy with the flowers, tipped over a large pitcher of water and broke the heads off some carnations. The trouble was, she was too preoccupied with a number of things to concentrate on what she was doing—with Sondra's threat to destroy Dain's manuscript, with the holiday in Paris (which seemed utterly unreal and reckless this morning), with Dain's opinion of Tony, and most of all with his behaviour last night.

At a little after twelve, with the shop full of customers, the telephone rang. Mrs Markham answered, and Fay heard her say in a chilly voice, 'You'll have to wait if you want to speak to Fay. She's busy. Perhaps I can take a message ... Oh, very well.'

She set down the receiver and told Fay with a smile that was completely false and purely for the benefit of the clientele, 'When you have a spare minute, dear, you're wanted on the telephone.'

It was Dain, Fay discovered some minutes later as she hurried over to the phone.

'Fay?'

'Yes. I'm very busy, Mr Legend.'

'So I gathered,' he said without apologising. 'After that—rather regrettable incident last night, I think we'd better meet and discuss your plans again. I take it you're free this afternoon? I suggest you drive over to Legend's Run——'

'That's impossible,' she said flatly and unhappily, aware that Mrs Markham was glaring at her. 'I'm doing something else.' It flitted through her mind that she could very easily go on to Legend's Run once she had seen Sondra, but Sondra would be livid and it was pointless to antagonise her.

'Then tomorrow,' he said, and she snapped back,

'I can't see you tomorrow either.'

'Too caught up with your boy-friend, are you? Very well. I'll be in Canberra on Tuesday. I'll see you after you finish work. We can have dinner together in some restaurant where things won't get out of hand—and talk in a civilised way. In the meantime you'd better get on with that typing.'

'I'll try,' she said evasively. 'Now I have to go——'

The result of that telephone call combined with the fact that the morning's work had been a disaster was inevitable. After she had locked the shop, Mrs Markham told her, 'I don't want you here on Monday, Fay—or on any day after that. I've had enough of your cavorting around. I don't know what your mother's going to think when she comes back and finds——'

Fay mentally blocked her ears. She simply didn't hear any more. Okay, she'd been late for work and someone had rung her up, but it wasn't all that bad. The fact was, Mrs Markham felt she was now too well off, and she preferred to have someone in the shop who was more submissive, more under her power. All the same, Fay was a little inclined to weep, and because of that she didn't trust herself enough to tell Mrs Markham she was sorry it had all ended like this. Mrs Markham handed her two weeks' wages and said a little tightly, 'I'm sorry you have nothing to say for yourself. If you'd apologised perhaps we could have tried again. You're young and the changes in your family fortune have evidently gone to your head, I realise that. I'd hoped you'd settle down when you saw I was taking your laxness seriously. It's all very unfortunate——'

Fay swallowed back her tears.

'I *am* sorry,' she blurted. 'But it just seems to have happened this way.'

'You don't want to make another effort, then?'

Fay shook her head. 'I—I may be going overseas,' she began, and her employer's face hardened instantly.

'Who on earth with? You can't go on your own—and that friend of yours, Dodie Hayes—last time you spoke of her she hadn't saved up anything like enough. Or do you expect your stepfather to fork out for the two of you?'

'Of course not,' Fay said slowly. She had a brief struggle with herself. If she was really going away with Tony—if she really believed she had nothing to be ashamed of—then she shouldn't be secretive. After a moment she told Mrs Markham, 'I'm going with Tony Thorpe, as a matter of fact, not with Dodie.'

Mrs Markham looked both shocked and affronted.

'You're going away with a *man*? You of all people! I'd never have believed it. I just don't know what your mother will think.'

'I'll write and tell my mother,' said Fay. 'Tony and I will just be travelling together, that's all. I like him very much, and as you said, I couldn't go on my own. But I'll be perfectly safe with him.' As she spoke, she remembered last night—Dain Legend saying, 'That's how safe you are with a man——' But with Tony, she would be safe.

'I give up,' sighed Mrs Markham. 'You've certainly changed, Fay. I suppose it's no use my offering you any advice, you wouldn't take it.'

When Fay left the shop, she found Tony waiting for her, and strangely her spirits sagged. Just at the moment everything seemed too much for her. He took her arm and looked at her with concern.

'Fay, you look washed out. What's up? Did I keep you out too late last night?'

She shook her head. 'I've just been given the sack.'

'Good lord! Why?' he asked as they began to walk along the street together.

'Oh, for being late—for not keeping my mind on my work.'

'Thinking of Paris,' he guessed, and she nodded unsmilingly. 'Well, it doesn't matter all that much, does it? You were going to quit work anyhow.'

'I suppose so,' she said, and added, 'But not for good.'

'Why not for good? Of course for good!' he exclaimed, then went on, 'What shall we do this afternoon? Suppose we have a meal and then drive out to the Cotter Dam. How does that sound?'

She shook her head. 'I'm sorry, Tony, I really can't come out with you this afternoon. I'd like to have lunch with you, but after that I—I have to go out somewhere.'

He stopped in the middle of the pavement and looked at her.

'You're not going out with another guy, are you, Fay?'

She flushed. 'Of course not!'

'Then what's more important than spending the rest of the day together? I thought you felt as I do——'

'I do,' she said vehemently. She didn't want to tell him about Sondra—the manuscript—all that sordid business. But he just couldn't come along with her. It wasn't possible. At last she said untruthfully, 'I have a long-standing engagement with—with a girl friend, that's all. I'd forgotten it. But please don't ask me to break it, Tony—it's just for the afternoon.'

His eyes looked into hers. They were very different from Dain Legend's eyes. Tony's eyes were blue, open, clear. There was no hardness and cynicism in them, they were friendly and frank, and she felt a little thrill and began to smile. He smiled too, then he put his arm around her and they walked on.

'All right ... You know, you're a fantastic girl, Fay,' he said, hugging her to him. 'Those eyes of yours—they're so candid, so honest. They're like a child's. I don't believe you could tell a lie if you tried.'

Fay laughed, but she felt uncomfortable. She'd just told a lie—and looked guileless as she did so. She didn't feel proud of herself, but she couldn't go back on it now.

Two and a half hours later she was driving along the Bungendore Road keeping an eye out for the turn-off Sondra had described to her. She found it at last, went through a gate and followed wheel tracks that ran along by a fence.

It was attractive country, but terribly dry just now. Rain was badly needed in the district and the grass was dry and straw-like. On the skyline the jagged scrawl of indigo mountains showed, the wheel tracks dipped down and around a long slope and Sondra's cottage came into view, partly hidden by big shade trees. Outside the garden fence Fay parked her car, then went through the garden to the house. It was very small, built of hand-hewn stone blocks with a verandah along the front.

Sondra came to the door when she knocked. She wore a simple dress of fine cotton in muted colours, and her golden hair hung down over her shoulders. She showed Fay into the sitting room. The cottage had obviously been restored and though it was small it was very attractive. Fay noticed some ceramic figures—a pair of swans, a cat, beautifully modelled and intriguingly glazed—and concluded that they must be Sondra's work.

'I suppose you want your packet,' the other girl said.

'Yes,' Fay agreed simply.

'And you're going to keep out of Dain's way?'

'As much as I can.'

'That's not good enough,' said Sondra, and Fay almost lost her temper.

'Honestly, Sondra, what do you expect me to do? You're welcome to all you want of Dain Legend—*I* don't want him. I can't think why you're so suspicious——'

'I'm suspicious because your precious mother's obviously trying to throw you into Dain's arms, and I'm not having it,' Sondra snapped.

Fay sighed. 'You're quite mistaken. And anyhow, I may be going away for a holiday soon—to Europe. With Tony Thorpe,' she concluded, thinking she might as well be honest. Soon everyone would know, at any rate; she hadn't exactly been keeping it to herself.

Sondra looked at her in silence for a long moment and then she laughed dryly. 'You *may*,' she said ironically. 'You've told Dain all about it, of course—there's nothing like a little drama to keep yourself in the forefront of his mind, is there? What's he going to do about it, I wonder? In his place, I'd let you have your head.'

'I'll do as I please regardless of his opinion,' Fay retorted. 'But as a matter of fact, he wants to discuss it with me on Tuesday night, so I'm afraid I just won't be able to keep out of his way on that occasion, Sondra.'

'And I'm sure you'll make the most of it,' Sondra snapped. 'All the same, you might discover Dain doesn't really care all that much who you go away with—or who you sleep with, either,' she added nastily.

'I'm not sleeping with anyone,' Fay said, flushing, and Sondra shrugged.

'I'm not interested in your morals. Frankly, I wouldn't be sorry if you disappeared from the scene. I can easily keep an eye on my father's apartment in Canberra—you're hardly a necessary adjunct to the family ... And by the way, there's something I want to talk to you about.' She hadn't asked Fay to sit down, and now she crossed to a small cedar desk and took a long business envelope from it. 'This account came in the mail the other day—addressed to my father. I believe he left you some money for various expenses?'

'Yes,' Fay agreed. 'Is it something I should pay?'

'You've guessed it in one,' said Sondra with a look of triumph. 'It's a bill for some of the refurnishing your mother talked Daddy into doing. I'll let you take care of it. It's fairly sizeable—four thousand-odd dollars.'

Fay blinked with shock. She was quite sure Walter

hadn't meant her to pay that bill, and Sondra must know it.

'Your father left five thousand dollars with me, Sondra,' she said. 'But it wasn't for that. I'm sure if he'd meant me to deal with a bill that size he'd have told me.'

'He told me,' said Sondra, raising her eyebrows. 'I can hardly be expected to pay it. What's bothering you, anyhow? Were you planning to keep the money as a nice little nest egg for yourself? Or to use it to take yourself off to Europe?'

'No, of course not,' Fay said stiffly. 'I can manage that for myself.'

'Then that's great. And Tony's not short of money, I'm sure. Isn't his father supposed to own a cattle station about the size of Belgium, up in the Northern Territory?'

'It's in Queensland,' Fay corrected her uncomfortably. 'And I don't imagine for a moment it's anything like as big as that.'

'No? Well, I'm only guessing ... Anyhow, here's the account for you to pay—and here's the manuscript you—lost,' Sondra added, taking the big envelope from a drawer in the writing desk. 'You must tell me all about your trip some time—or is it all in the air still?'

'More or less,' Fay said aloofly. Deliberately, she opened the envelope Sondra had handed her and checked the contents.

'It's all present and correct,' Sondra said. 'I hope you're not planning to visit Legend's Run now you've got it back. Because I don't want you to, do you see? I'll be going there myself when you've gone, and I'll tell Dain you found his manuscript on the floor of your car, shall I?'

'No, thank you. You needn't bother telling him anything,' Fay said. 'And I wasn't going to see him—I'm going back to Canberra to make a start on this typing. I want to finish it by Tuesday so I can give it to Dain then. And I'm going out tonight.'

'With Tony? Well, have a good time, won't you? And if you want to invite him back to the flat, go ahead. I shan't be there tonight.'

Fay seethed inwardly but didn't retort. She was thankful to get back in her car and drive away.

CHAPTER FIVE

FAY spent the remainder of the weekend with Tony. On Sunday they drove out to the Tidbinbilla Nature Reserve, parked the car, then followed the Lyrebird Trail. It went through manna gums and blackwoods, and through the bush they heard the call of the lyrebirds. They picnicked on the ridge and talked about themselves. Fay learned that Tony was an only child and that his mother was dead. He told her something about the work a jackeroo did on a big cattle station, and talked about the Boss, as he called his father, and his stocking policies. Listening, Fay thought how wrong Dain Legend was in trying to make her doubt him.

'What's the name of your father's cattle station, Tony?' she asked curiously.

'Confetti Downs.' His blue eyes met hers smilingly. 'But don't ask me why. It could have something to do with a wedding there in the early days, or it could be an anglicised version of some aboriginal word. When you come up there—we'll see if we can root out the meaning.'

More than a little thrilled, Fay agreed.

Afterwards they went down through the peppermint gums and by a different way back to the car, and as they drove back to Canberra Tony asked, 'Dinner?'

'I don't think so,' Fay said reluctantly. 'I'm tired, and I have some typing to do.'

'Then tomorrow,' he said, looking disappointed. 'We'll meet in town, shall we? And—er—you haven't forgotten about that loan, have you?'

'No, I haven't forgotten,' Fay said a little hesitantly.

'But can't they wait a little longer at the travel agency? I'd rather not go into town tomorrow. I've made up my mind to get this typing off my hands and—well, I was going to ask if you could possibly wait till Wednesday.' She glanced at his profile as she spoke and saw a slight frown crease his brows before he said lightly,

'Okay. My own money might have arrived by then. Meanwhile, I'll chat up the girl in the travel agency and see what that accomplishes.'

Fay felt relieved. Maybe it was absurd to be so determined she would do the typing, but she didn't like the idea of Sondra getting away with threats, and anyhow, once it was done and handed over, Dain would no longer have any excuse for pestering her.

She worked hard that night despite her tiredness, and again the following day. Tony rang the flat and asked her to have dinner with him on Monday night, but took it goodnaturedly when she said no. He wasn't quite as unmoved when she refused him the following night as well, and she didn't tell him she was meeting Dain Legend.

All Tuesday she was on edge waiting for the telephone to ring, certain that Dain would have rung Hearts and Flowers to make arrangements about meeting her—and discovered she had got the sack. But he didn't telephone. She finished typing the manuscript and was pleased with the neat job she had made of it. She had found the subject matter interesting and even felt curious to see the homestead on Legend's Run. But she could live without that pleasure, seeing she would have to endure more of Dain Legend's company to attain it.

When she hadn't heard from him by four-thirty, she dialled his number at Legend's Run. The telephone rang and rang and no one answered it, and she could only conclude he had left already and planned to pick her up at the flower shop—in which case she'd better get a move on!

She hurried through a shower, then got into a black crêpe suit that had been her mother's. It was simple and elegant, but Claire had put on a little too much weight to wear the skirt. Instead of wearing a blouse, she tied a silk scarf, black and splashed with yellow and violet, at the neckline. She fastened tiny black and gold earrings in her lobes, used her mother's Chanel, her blusher, and the mauvish eye-shadow she had borrowed before. She had washed her hair and blow-dried it, and it was at its best. 'You're not without physical attraction,' Dain had said——

She cut off her thoughts suddenly. Anyone would think she was looking forward to this date, but it wasn't a date at all. It was a—business meeting. She knew very well Dain was going to do all he could to stop her going away with Tony. Yet what *could* he do?

She stood back and looked at herself full length in the long wardrobe mirror. She looked good—she also looked decidedly more than twenty. He would hardly be able to say she looked more like sixteen tonight.

As she went down to the street in the elevator she was aware that she was far from certain she was going to get the better of him. He was the tough, unscrupulous kind of man who usually got his own way if he had made up his mind about it, and she couldn't help suspecting he'd find some way to twist her arm so she couldn't possibly go away. Well, at least the tickets hadn't been paid for, she thought wryly, and wondered if that had been—just a little—in her mind when she had put off making Tony the loan until after her meeting with Dain.

Some minutes later, as she drove down Northbourne Avenue towards Civic, she thought of one way Dain could—blackmail her. He could threaten to let her mother know what she was doing—the way *he* saw it.

She had no doubt he would find a way of getting in touch with Claire if he chose to do so. And the result would be that Claire would believe him and would come hurrying home, her honeymoon—her world tour—ruined. Rather than let that happen, obviously, she would have to give in. She wouldn't go to Paris or anywhere else with Tony.

Would she mind so terribly? Strangely, she wasn't sure that she would. It had all happened so suddenly, and it was—it was a crazy thing to do, really. Though she would never admit that to Dain Legend...

She parked her car and went straight to Hearts and Flowers. He wasn't outside waiting for her, and though the shop was closed, through the window she could see Mrs Markham still moving about.

Fay tapped on the glass, Mrs Markham looked up, and seeing her, came to open the door.

'Well, hello, Fay! What is it?' She took in her get-up, and Fay knew she was surprised at her sophisticated appearance and was probably satisfied she had been right about the change in her.

'I was wondering if Mr Legend—my—guardian—had rung the shop today,' she said after she had greeted her ex-employer. 'I—I haven't let him know yet that I'm not working here any more.'

'No. There've been no phone calls for you. What's the trouble? Were you meeting him tonight?'

'Yes. I—we arranged it over the phone on Saturday morning.'

'Well, I'm afraid I can't help you,' Mrs Markham said definitely, then softened enough to offer, 'Use the phone if you like.'

Fay shook her head. 'It doesn't matter, thank you. He's probably waiting for me at the hotel. I just thought I'd—check up here first... Has Judy started work?'

'She has indeed. She's very happy to have the job ... Now if you don't mind I want to finish clearing up. I hope you find your guardian, Fay. You're certainly dressed all ready for an important date, aren't you? Didn't I say you'd be into expensive clothes at any tick of the clock?'

'Yes, you did, Mrs Markham.' Fay coloured with annoyance. 'But this suit was my mother's—she gave it to me months ago. It's not new.'

Did Mrs Markham believe that? Well, what did it matter? She left the shop and walked away quickly in the direction of the hotel where Dain had taken her to lunch that day. Not that she really thought he'd be there, but she didn't know what else to do. She had his manuscript and the typing she had done carefully wrapped in brown paper, and she had been all keyed up for this meeting. Now her cheeks felt hot and she was getting flustered. She simply couldn't understand his not getting in touch with her. Surely he couldn't be standing her up! She couldn't believe it. Not of Dain Legend. Not when he'd as good as ordered her to meet him, and was so drastically intent on preventing her from doing what she was planning. Now it began to look as though he didn't really care after all whether she went away with Tony or not.

And here she was, all dressed up.

Furious with him, and furious with herself as well, she looked into the hotel lounge, went into the restaurant, came out to the lobby again. Then, hurrying, she went back to Hearts and Flowers.

He wasn't there.

'I *hate* him,' she thought, almost in tears. That he should treat her like this—so contemptuously—as though she didn't matter——

Fuming, she walked to the car park. He *could* have stopped her going away with Tony if he'd really wanted to, she thought illogically. As it was, nothing was going to stop her. Her mother would discover how mistaken she had been in entrusting her daughter to a man like him! She never wanted to see him again. She'd post his rotten manuscript off to him tomorrow and she'd have no more to do with him. She'd go to Sydney with Tony just as soon as they'd paid for their tickets.

She drove home dangerously fast, garaged her car, and only then noticed there was a light in her apartment. *Sondra,* she thought, her heart like lead. Damn! That was absolutely the last straw! She wished she had stayed in town and had something to eat—gone to a movie—rung up Dodie Hayes. Well, she wasn't going to put in the evening with her stepsister. She hoped Sondra was going out.

Sondra came into the hall when she unlocked the front door and went in.

'Fay! Where on earth have you been, all dressed up like a dog's dinner?' she queried rudely. 'Oh, of course, I remember—you were meeting Dain tonight, weren't you? It must have been short and sweet,' she added maliciously. Then, her eyes going to the brown paper packet Fay was carrying, 'Didn't your typing pass muster? Or have you taken on another lot?'

If Fay had thought vaguely of pretending she had seen Dain, she changed her mind. After all, the fewer lies she told the better. She brushed past Sondra and looked into the sitting room—almost as if she expected to find Dain sitting on the sofa there. She didn't, of course, and she asked jerkily, 'He—Dain—didn't telephone? Or call in here for me?'

Sondra looked mystified. 'Here? No ... Good heavens, do you mean he didn't turn up? So that's why you're back so early! Well, I'm not terribly surprised. You do have a rather inflated idea of the extent of his interest in you.'

'Oh, for goodness' sake!' Fay exclaimed. 'You know very well why we were meeting. You know he wanted to talk to me about—about Tony.'

Sondra looked her over deliberately, her glance lingering on the little earrings, her make-up, the smart suit and high-heeled shoes. Her nostrils twitched slightly as if she recognised the scent of Chanel, then she laughed briefly.

'You really amuse me with your protests, Fay—and those angelic eyes of yours. I've never seen you so tarted up, and don't tell me it wasn't for Dain's benefit ... I hope you paid that account, by the way.'

'I didn't,' Fay snapped. 'I haven't been in town this week. But don't worry—I'll pay up, your father's money's still there. And if you think I've been—splurging out and buying clothes for Dain's benefit, you can think again. I've had this outfit for months.'

'I don't believe it,' Sondra said calmly. She wasn't nearly so polite as Mrs Markham. 'Anyone can see you're out to impress Dain. I expect you're trying to make him jealous, pretending you're going away with Tony Thorpe. Personally, I don't believe for a moment that Tony will take you to Europe—and I told Dain so. You may as well know Dain finds you a pain in the neck with your idiotic behaviour. And if that's hard to take, it's too bad. I at least am aware he has enough to do without having you constantly pestering him and trading on the fact he told your mother he'd keep an eye on you.'

So Sondra had told him that Fay wasn't going away with Tony—and for that reason, he hadn't bothered keeping his appointment with her! Fay was ready to cry with temper and humiliation, but she wasn't going to let herself go in front of Sondra. Her eyes smouldering, she merely said, 'If he wasn't coming in to town he should have let me know.'

'The point might be made better this way,' Sondra said icily. 'You don't interest him as a woman, Fay— you're not his type.'

'I don't want to be his type,' Fay said wearily. 'And if you only knew, he's been pestering me rather than the other way about. I mean, he's always telling me what I should and shouldn't do,' she added hastily in case Sondra should take her remark to mean something else. 'I only wish he'd never agreed to be my guardian.'

'I assure you he wishes the same thing,' said Sondra, tossing back her hair. 'I'll be going back to the cottage tomorrow. I'll let him know how upset you were about his not turning up, shall I?'

'I'm not upset,' snapped Fay, her colour high. 'If he considers his obligation to me is ended then that suits me just fine. What you *can* tell him is that—that Tony and I are going to Paris. I've left my job and we've got the tickets.' So much for *your* scepticism! she thought with a slight feeling of triumph as Sondra stared at her unbelievingly. She turned on her heel and went to her bedroom.

Now she'd burned her boats, she thought, sinking down in the bedroom chair. She would make a liar of herself if she didn't go now. In fact, it looked as if she would more or less have to go. She frowned. *Have* to go? What was wrong with her, thinking like that? Didn't she still think it—romantic, daring, unreal? Wasn't she falling more and more in love with Tony every time she saw him? Of course she was, she told herself firmly. She was glad she had told Sondra she was going—and asked her to pass on the news to Dain. She was glad too that he hadn't turned up tonight and spoilt everything, as he undoubtedly would have.

Sondra left for the cottage the next day. Fay heard nothing from Dain and didn't expect to hear anything.

Well, the pain in the neck would very soon be right off his hands.

She paid the furniture bill and took the money from her personal account so Tony could pay for their return flights to Paris. His money hadn't yet come through from Queensland, but he expected it at any time. She was left with fifty-one dollars in her own account and two hundred and thirteen in the account Walter had opened in her name. Before she left, she would possibly withdraw it all. Since Dain Legend hadn't been in touch with her, she posted off the work she had done for him plus his handwritten manuscript, but she didn't enclose a message of any kind and she didn't mention payment. His silence she answered with silence.

Tony had decided they would fly to Sydney as soon as his money arrived, which it apparently did on Friday, for on that day he dashed around fixing hotel bookings and a number of other details, leaving Fay free to meet Dodie Hayes and let her know what was happening.

'You're really going?' Dodie breathed, eyes wide, as they sat in a small café near Garema Place. 'Oh, Fay, how fabulous! It's like a dream—the sort of thing that never really happens. Well, not to people you know. Aren't you at all scared, going away with a man? But I guess it's different when you're in love. Are you going to marry him?'

'I expect so,' said Fay, though she was talking off the top of her head, she really had no idea. 'He's going to manage the outstation at Confetti Downs this year, so I guess—well, maybe he wants to settle down. I'll send you a postcard from Paris, anyhow, Dodie.'

Dodie giggled. 'Paris! Maybe you'll get married there. You look so pretty since you had your hair cut, Fay... Have you written to your mother? What does she think?'

'I'll write before we leave,' said Fay. 'I know she'd like Tony—but I expect she'll be rather surprised,' she finished inadequately.

'I guess so!' Dodie agreed.

On Saturday afternoon Fay and Tony boarded the plane for Sydney. Fay had packed warm clothes for Paris, summer clothes for Sydney. In cash, she had with her just over two hundred dollars, which was all she had until Tony paid back the loan for his fare. Flying out from Canberra, she tried to tell herself she was happy and excited, but deep down she was disturbed. She had written to her mother the day before and then hadn't posted the letter. No matter how she put it, she couldn't make what she was doing sound even the smallest bit sensible, nor could she make her love for Tony seem real. As for Dain, she just hadn't been able to tell any tales about him at all. Right up to the last minute, at the airport, she had half expected him to turn up and drag her back to town, but he hadn't.

She glanced nervously at the man beside her and began to think about what was ahead of her. Had he booked separate rooms for them at the hotel? She longed to ask him, but somehow she couldn't bring herself to do so.

He hadn't booked separate rooms. They had a suite with twin beds and a handsome bathroom. Under other circumstances, Fay might have been dashing around examining the fittings—looking through the window at the park across the street, exclaiming over the size of the bathroom. But as it was, once they were alone with their luggage, she had a fit of shyness.

'What's up?' asked Tony as she stood in the middle of the bedroom doing nothing. 'Don't you like it?'

'Yes, but—you didn't ask me if—if I minded sharing,' she blurted out.

He crossed the room to her quickly and took her

hands in his. 'You didn't think we'd have separate rooms, did you?' he said, his voice soft. 'Not feeling the way we do about each other——'

She said indistinctly, 'I hadn't really—thought about it.'

'You hadn't? Well, I had. But don't worry, we're going to have a great time together, Fay. I've got seats for a concert at the Opera House tonight, and absolutely all you have to do is enjoy yourself and leave everything to me ... Why don't you unlock your bag and find something really super to wear tonight, then take a shower and think of the fun we're going to have. I'll look after you, I promise.'

Fay took a shower, and under it she relaxed. He wasn't like Dain Legend. She would never have been able to share a suite with *him* and not be scared out of her wits. But she wasn't afraid of Tony. Some men were decent even if others were brutes.

They did have fun that night. They ate in style in the hotel restaurant, then took a taxi to the Opera House. Oh, the lights on the dark harbour, the warm flowing air of the summer night, the stars swinging brilliantly in the black pool of the sky! Tony looked dashing in his dark suit and white shirt, and Fay wore the black crêpe suit that had been Claire's, and deliberately didn't think of the last time she had worn it. Tony said she looked like a million dollars.

They went straight back to the hotel after the concert. Tony went to the lounge to get himself a nightcap, and Fay went to bed. She didn't even hear him when he came up later, she was fast asleep.

On Sunday they walked round Hyde Park, lunched in town, then went down to Circular Quay and took a long and delightful harbour cruise. At night they went to a movie, and as they went back to the hotel, Tony talked about Paris and the exciting things they would do there. He had been overseas before—to Florence and Venice and Paris too.

'But this time will be different, because I'm going with you,' he said.

When Fay came out from the shower that night he had had his nightcap and come back to the suite. He had turned all the lights off except one, and he was sitting on her bed, fully dressed. Fay's heart gave a frightened lurch as she met his eyes, and she looked away quickly and told him, 'I want to get into bed, Tony.'

He got up at once, but when she reached her bed and sat on it to take her slippers off, he sat down again, very close to her. She smelled the alcohol on his breath as he put his arm around her and pulled her against him, kissing her neck and feeling for the elastic of her pyjama waistband. Fay pulled away from him, shocked by her feeling of distaste, and slid off the bed to stand trembling, her back against the wall. He looked up at her smiling slightly and she was very much aware of his good looks. Yet she didn't want him to make love to her, she felt she would run screaming from the room if he tried. Unexpectedly her mind presented her with a picture of Dain Legend, his mouth cruel as he held her against his bare chest, bruised her mouth with his kisses, and made her physically aware of every part of him. 'I could rape you here and now if I wanted to,' he had said. And she had told him afterwards, 'Tony's not like you——'

Now, tremblingly, she looked at Tony through her lashes and tried to swallow down her feeling of panic. *Was* he like that?

Still smiling, still sitting on her bed, he leaned back on his hands, then he said softly, casually, 'No?'

Fay was so relieved she could have cried. Her mouth trembled as she smiled back at him and shook her head.

'No.' No sex, because no love. Elementary, my dear Watson. The ridiculous words came into her head.

Tony got up from her bed and she watched him go to the other side of the room and pull the quilt from his bed. He was—civilised. So Dain Legend was wrong. Tony *wasn't* like him. She was perfectly safe with him—as safe as she chose to be.

Yet however safe she felt, deep down she was beginning to regret she had started this adventure. It was too late to go back now, she had taken the first irrevocable steps and she had to go on. Perhaps, she thought, getting into bed and lying on her side, perhaps it would all come out all right. Perhaps proximity would work its magic—she would fall deeply in love with Tony—they would marry, go to Confetti Downs, and live happily ever after.

Somehow, tonight, she didn't believe a word of it. She couldn't imagine sleeping with him. And she had no idea why.

On Monday, he suggested she should go shopping while he fixed some details of their stay in Paris. Fay agreed, though she had no intention of doing any shopping. She didn't, at the moment, have all that much money to throw around and she wondered if she should say anything about the loan she had made him that had left her so short of funds. It would be weak not to, and before they parted outside the hotel she forced herself to mention it.

'Tony—about that money I lent you. For your fare, I mean——'

He smiled down into her eyes. 'I haven't forgotten, Fay. Tomorrow we'll buy our travellers' cheques and we'll sort it all out then. Okay?'

She nodded, he kissed her and said softly, 'We'll talk money tonight.'

They didn't talk money until after dinner—a dinner

that took them to nearly ten o'clock. Then, back in their suite, Tony wanted to know what shopping she had done.

'None,' she admitted. 'I just window-shopped.'

'I thought women liked to buy clothes. Or are you waiting till you get to Paris?' he teased.

'No. I just don't need anything,' she said with a smile.

'Oh, come on now! Then what about a camera? You should have bought one duty-free to pick up at the airport.'

'I didn't think of it,' she said awkwardly.

'Then we'll buy a couple tomorrow,' he said. 'And see about our travellers' cheques, of course. You did have the bank send your signature down to Sydney like I told you, I hope.'

'No. I brought all my money with me,' she confessed. She was sitting on the end of her bed feeling tired and somehow confused,

'You brought it with you? For God's sake——' Tony, who was removing his tie, looked round at her frowningly. 'Then how much do you have in cash?'

'About two hundred dollars.'

He stared at her in amazement. '*What?* What on earth are you talking about? *All* your money, didn't you say?—and now you tell me—— Come on, Fay, you must be joking!'

'I'm not,' she said flushing. 'I don't have any more than that, Tony—except the money I lent you.'

He continued to stare at her, and suddenly his clear blue eyes were cold and hostile, the eyes of a stranger. 'What about the money Walter Marshall put in your bank account? A crazy amount, didn't you say?'

The blood had gone from Fay's face leaving it pale. 'It was five thousand dollars,' she said quietly. 'It's—there's none of that left. I had a big account to pay before we left Canberra—for the furnishing in the flat.'

'My—God!' he exclaimed. 'You talked as if you had a fortune. Five thousand dollars! And now you have two hundred dollars left! What exactly do you plan to do with that?'

Fay couldn't speak. She was shocked to the very marrow of her bones by the change in him. Finally she said shakily, 'It's—enough for my needs, Tony. And after all, you have——' Her voice trailed off into silence. What did he have—apart from the money she had loaned him? She no longer knew.

He began unbuttoning his shirt, his face expressionless, and after a moment Fay picked up her pyjamas and went into the shower.

They didn't discuss the matter further. In bed, in the dark, she lay awake. Dain had said Tony was a fortune-hunter, and she had been so very sure he was wrong. Now she didn't know. Had he been counting on Walter Marshall's money to finance this—holiday?

She heard him turn over, and she said into the darkness, 'Is it too late to—to cancel my flight, Tony?'

'Oh, go to sleep,' he mumbled. 'We'll talk things over tomorrow.'

CHAPTER SIX

FAY woke late the next morning, dragging herself out of a deep sleep to become aware of an odd silence, a stillness about her.

She sat up in bed and stared around the room. Tony had gone. And so had all his clothes, all his luggage. There was not a sign that he had ever been there. Her heart pounded, and her thoughts lurched crazily back to their conversation of the night before, a conversation concerned totally with money. So Dain was right: it had been the Marshall money and not Fay Douglas that had attracted Tony. Once he discovered she had practically nothing, he had left her. There was to be no holiday in Paris.

She leaped out of bed and found her handbag, and opened it with trembling fingers. Thank God, what little money she had was still there. But the loan she had made him—it looked as though she wouldn't see that again.

Oh, what a fool she'd been, to be so stupidly credulous! She hoped, though without much optimism, that at least he had paid the hotel bill.

He hadn't, she discovered half an hour later, and the money she had was not nearly enough to cover it. Idiotically, she thought of ringing Dain Legend and asking him, 'Please send me the money to pay a big hotel bill—to get back home, to support me till I find another job.' He was supposed to be there if she needed help, wasn't he? But of course she wouldn't ring him, not in a fit, and rather illogically she reflected that if only he had kept his appointment with her last week, she wouldn't be in such a predicament now. But it was no use blaming Dain, and instead of wasting her time in futile regrets she had better decide what she was going to do.

The only thing she could think of was to ring Dodie Hayes this evening, when she would be home from work. Dodie had enough savings to come to her rescue, and she would be able to repay her once her mother came home. Fay sat in the hotel bedroom feeling appalled. 'I can't go back to Canberra,' she thought miserably. Have Sondra know. Worse, have Dain know. Strangely, that upset her more than Tony's desertion of her. In a way, she was glad to be rid of him, though it hurt that he had made such a fool of her. She despised herself for her gullibility. She had really thought he was in love with her, that she had flattened him when she smiled at him that first day they met in the shop. Instead, what had attracted him was the fact she was Sondra's stepsister; it was as plain as daylight now. Yet why did he want her money? The answer to that seemed pretty obvious. His story about Confetti Downs hadn't been true. And she had swallowed it whole. What a fool!

'I won't tell Dain Legend a *thing*,' she thought fiercely. 'Just that I changed my mind.' He needn't ever know that she had been taken for a ride, lost all her money. He could *think* what he liked, but he would never really know.

Yet, knowing Dain Legend she was miserably sure he would force the truth out of her somehow.

She put in a long day wandering round the city. She ate a chocolate bar for lunch and spent most of the afternoon sitting in Centrepoint looking out at the city street and seeing nothing. Finally she returned to the hotel suite to telephone Dodie. She had just reached out for the receiver when the phone rang, startling her badly in her nervous state.

FIRST PASSION

'Hello?' she said, her voice shaking.

'Fay?'

Oh God! It was Dain Legend's voice. Fay almost passed out. 'Yes,' she quavered.

'It's Dain Legend here. I'll be along to see you in five minutes.'

'Where are you?' she asked, but before the words were out of her mouth he rang off. Bang!

Fay hung up, and stood there, her heart beating fast. Dain was here, in Sydney, and, obviously, right in this very hotel. In five minutes he would be at her door. Oh no! It was too much!

She stared around at the litter of clothes she hadn't repacked, the mess on the chest under the mirror, the signs of disorder that seemed to symbolise her state of mind, then she rushed to the mirror. She looked ravaged—dark under the eyes, no colour in her cheeks. Even her hair looked lifeless, and needed brushing. Frantically, she used lipstick, grabbed up her brush, threw her pyjamas into her suitcase. What on earth was she going to tell him? How much did he already know? Everything, of course—except what had happened this morning.

'What do you want?' she asked abruptly when she opened the door to him exactly five minutes after his phone call.

'What do you think I want? To break up your idyll, of course, even though it may be a little late in the day.' He pushed her aside and moved into the room. 'Where's your boy-friend?'

Where was her boy-friend? Fay hadn't the slightest idea in the world, and she wanted to laugh hysterically. Instead, and quite unexpectedly, she burst into tears, rushed to her bed, and threw herself on it, face down.

A moment later she felt the movement of the mattress as Dain sat on the side of the bed near her.

'Well, where is he?' She had never heard a voice so harsh and unsympathetic. It made her curl up inside, stopped the flow of her tears as nothing else could have done. Female tears apparently didn't reach the heart of a man like Dain Legend—probably because he didn't have a heart. She dried her eyes furiously on a corner of the bedspread and sat up. His black eyes looked at her implacably and she hated him anew for his maleness and his arrogance. He despised her. Oh, how she wished she hadn't burst into tears! But she had just lost control.

She glared back at him and said, 'Where do you think he is? Can't you see for yourself? He's—he's gone.' She gestured futilely around the room—to the other bed—and the minute she did so a little chill went through her. How ingenuous could you be! Now she had admitted quite unnecessarily that they had been sharing this suite, and her face crimsoned guiltily.

She saw his lip curl, and his eyes grew colder and angrier.

'When did he leave you?'

It was a direct question, and if she answered it she would be telling him too much. She hadn't meant to tell him a thing, but how on earth was she to get out of it, now he was here? She could hardly say she had changed her mind, as she had planned—not after weeping the way she had. Uncertainly she tried it anyhow.

'Who—who said he'd left me? I—I changed my mind about going to Paris, that's all.'

One eyebrow went up sceptically as he felt for cigarettes and lit one.

'Exactly what made you do that, I wonder? Did you at last discover he was more interested in your bank account than in your pretty figure? My God, I ought to give you a beating here and now to teach you to listen to your elders and betters in future!'

'You won't touch me!' she flared, moving along the bed away from him.

Dain drew on his cigarette and looked at her through narrowed eyes.

'Don't be too sure of that. I've several good reasons for wanting to teach you a lesson. I agreed to be your protector with the best intentions in the world, you know—though I certainly didn't realise what a menace you'd prove to be. I did expect more co-operation than to have you walk out on me as you did, though, particularly when Sondra explained the circumstances.'

Fay's eyes widened with hostility. He certainly had a hide! He didn't turn up for the appointment *he'd* made, and then he accused her of walking out. He hadn't even made any effort to contact her afterwards—and what had Sondra explained? That he thought Fay a pain in the neck—that he was busy enough without having her on his hands ... ?

'You want it all your own way, don't you?' she accused. 'You didn't really care what I did, and I can't think why you're bothering about me now.'

'And nor can I,' he snapped. 'I've had the devil's own job tracking you down in the few hours since I've been back from Melbourne. I can assure you I wasn't in the mood for a game of hide-and-seek, either.'

So he'd been in Melbourne—visiting his ex-wife again, she thought resentfully.

'I wasn't playing hide-and-seek,' she retorted. 'I didn't make a secret of—of what I was doing.'

'Oh, quit putting on an act! You know damned well it was all in the air last time I spoke to you about it,' he said tersely. 'I finally contacted your friend Dodie Hayes with Mrs Markham's help. She seemed the only person who had an inkling of where you were off to. No one else knew a thing, including Sondra, which I consider pretty poor. I hardly expected to find you still here, and I can tell you I wasn't looking forward to chasing you halfway across the world.'

'As if you would have!' Fay scoffed, chafing at what he had said about Sondra, because she certainly hadn't left her entirely in the dark. 'How long were you away in Melbourne, anyhow?'

He looked at her sharply. 'I left on the Sunday night. I tried to telephone you in the afternoon, but presumably you were out with your boy-friend, so I had to leave it to Sondra to explain. I took it for granted you'd have the decency to wait till I came back before rushing into something you knew I disapproved of so strongly.'

'Did you? Well, I—I didn't think it mattered particularly whether you disapproved or not,' said Fay. She was disconcerted to know he had sent her a message about the dinner date after all. And that Sondra simply hadn't passed it on. Her stepsister certainly knew how to play dirty! But there seemed little point in telling tales on her at this stage of the game. It wouldn't change anything.

Dain got up from the bed and paced across the room to pick up an ashtray, then come back to her.

'What are you planning to do now you've been disillusioned about Tony Thorpe?'

'Who says I have been?' she countered, then added quickly, 'I suppose I'm coming home, that's all.'

'You suppose so, do you? And how long is it going to take you to be certain about it?'

Fay bit her lip. She was stuck with an unalterable, unhideable fact. She couldn't go back to Canberra until she had paid her hotel bill, and she couldn't do that until she got hold of some more money. She looked at her fingernails. 'I am certain. I just have to—to arrange something with someone first,' she said vaguely.

Plainly, she had infuriated him. He put his cigarette in the ashtray he was holding, thrust it down on the bedside table, and almost in the same movement pulled her to her feet and shook her.

'What the hell are you talking about? Now come on, I want facts and figures, not inanities. What's this all about? You're arranging exactly what—and with whom?'

His fingers were hurting her and tears had started to her eyes, both because of this and because of his tone. She tried to twist free of him, but the only result was that he held her more inescapably. Brute strength. She thought of Tony from whom she had escaped so easily the other night when they had been on this bed together. She had been safe then, but she wasn't now.

'Let go! You're hurting me!'

'Then answer my question. What are you up to?'

'Nothing,' she stammered, then suddenly she went limp, and gave in. 'I'm not up to anything,' she said sullenly. 'I need some money, that's all. To pay the hotel bill, and—and until I find another job.'

'And now,' he said, his voice dead level, 'tell me why you don't have any money.'

Of course, he had to know it all, she thought bitterly.

'Why do you think?' she said. 'You're so smart. You—*you* told me Tony only wanted——' She stopped to bite back her tears of humiliation, then forced herself to go on. 'But it needn't concern you. Dodie will lend me some money.'

He thrust her from him abruptly and she fell back on the bed.

'So you gave him the lot. My God, what a besotted little fool! I just hope you've learned your lesson!'

'Oh, don't pretend you care,' she said, struggling to her feet. 'You probably think it serves me right. You've never liked me. And—and I object to being pushed around like that,' she finished angrily.

'It may be the only way to get any sense out of you,'

he grated. 'Well, you're not borrowing money from Dodie Hayes, and I'm not going to lend you a cent either. You're not to be trusted. I've failed to control you on your credulous mother's behalf and I'm not taking any more chances, though God knows it's like shutting the stable door after the horse has been stolen ... You're coming back with me to Legend's Run where you'll be right under my nose.'

'What?' Fay's face paled. 'I'm—I'm certainly not! And you can't make me.'

'Can't I?' he said unpleasantly. 'Perhaps you'd rather I cabled your mother the sordid details of your recent behaviour. Running away with a man you've barely met—losing your virginity to him as well as you money——'

'You wouldn't!' Fay exclaimed, her voice low and quivering. 'That—that would be contemptible and—and not true. Tony's not—not like that at all. He's——'

He broke in contemptuously, 'Who do you think you're fooling this time, Fay? I'm right here to see the end of your adventure, and I can guess what went on. I hope you're not going to tell me you're still in love with the bastard. He's left you, hasn't he? And taken your money. So don't start protecting him.'

'I'm protecting myself,' she said hotly, 'And I—I wish you'd get out of my room. I don't need your help—I can ring Dodie.'

'I'm dictating the terms,' Dain said flatly. 'You'll do as I say or I promise I'll send your parents such an earful they'll be back on the next jet flight. Your days of freedom are over. You can settle down and do some work for me at Legend's Run. You're a competent enough typist, and it will at least—keep you off the streets,' he finished, his mouth twisting cynically.

Fay gasped, 'Don't dare to speak to me like that! You're insufferable. You won't let me say a word for myself.'

'Calm down,' he advised. 'You can do all the talking you like once you're at Legend's Run—and that's where you're going whether you like it or not.'

Fay had no choice and she knew it. She said below her breath, 'All right. And now will you please go away and let me have some peace?'

'I'm afraid not,' he said disagreeably. 'I'll give you a choice, Fay. You can leave for Canberra with me right away—allowing you time to pack up, of course. Or you and I will share this room tonight.'

She stared at him stupefied. 'What—what do you mean?'

'I mean I don't trust you, that I'm not giving you a chance to do another disappearing act. What did you think I meant?' His eyes looked mockingly into hers and she blushed scarlet and turned away from him quickly.

'I'll come now,' she said shakily.

'Fine. Then start packing.'

He lit another cigarette and sat down to watch her.

Fay had plenty of time as they drove south in Dain's car that night to think of what was ahead of her, and she scarcely spoke to him all the way. She hated him for his judgment of her, yet she knew she had brought it on herself. How could she convince him she hadn't slept with Tony when he knew they had shared a room? She knew very well that if Dain had been the man in the case he would certainly have made love to her. She wouldn't have had one chance in a million of escaping him. The thought made her shiver, and her reflections went to Legend's Run. How safe was she going to be there, more or less alone with him, she presumed. She supposed he must have a housekeeper, and Sondra—oh, Sondra would be dropping in often, of that she was in no doubt. Sondra wouldn't like her being there—not one little bit, but despite her stepsister's threats, there was nothing Fay could do about the situation.

She asked aloud, as they turned off the Bungendore Road, 'What will you tell Sondra about my coming here?' She looked at his profile in the light from the dashboard and found it hard and aloof. It was late and she was overtired. They had had coffee and sandwiches in Mittagong, though she had managed to get down only a very little food in her state of nerves, and all she longed for now was sleep.

He flicked her a glance. 'You mean, am I going to tell Sondra that your lover walked out on you? I'll leave it to you, Fay. You can tell her whatever you like, but don't be surprised if you find she's guessed how your escapade ended. She made her own assessment of Tony Thorpe some time ago.'

Oh dear, yes, Fay thought bitterly. Sondra was clever, she was really clued up. But that pain in the neck, Fay Douglas—she didn't know what she was doing. She fell into every pitfall that was ever laid, and she'd fallen into one right now, going to Legend's Run with Dain Legend.

His house, she discovered, was gracious even if he wasn't. A mile-long drive, winding through giant kurrajongs and box trees, ended at a handsome gate that shone white in the starlight. The silence was deep and the air so mellow it could have been heaven she was going to instead of purgatory. The great pines around the parklike lawns and the long low white house made dark shadows as she approached the wide verandah with Dain, crossed its polished hardwood floor and went inside.

She followed him down a wide hall and he opened a door.

'You can have this room, Fay.' He switched on an

apricot-shaded lamp, and a spacious bedroom with a comfortable-looking three-quarter bed was softly illuminated. Dain took hold of the end of the heavy white crocheted bedspread and flung it back, revealing a sprigged sheet turned back over a pale lemon cotton blanket. 'The bed's all ready—I guess you're tired.'

He disappeared and she looked around her. She had pictured herself coming to prison, but it was a beautiful room, with good vibes, she thought absently, moving to the french doors and looking across the verandah through wistaria leaves into the starlit night. Another world. A world that could be beautiful if you belonged in it.

She was hanging her clothes in the roomy cedar wardrobe when Dain reappeared and from the door tossed two pale yellow towels on to the bed.

'There's a bathroom two doors along,' he told her. 'Turn left when you come out your door. Goodnight.'

Maybe she was confused, but ten minutes later, in her dressing gown with her towel and bathroom things in her arms, she opened a door and found herself in his bedroom. He was in his shorts and nothing else, and Fay was so shocked she stood frozen, mentally accusing him of deliberately giving her wrong directions. His black eyes raked her glitteringly, lingering where the satin gown clung to the smooth rounded line of her hips and breast.

'What's your problem?' he demanded, pacing towards her lithe as a leopard. 'Do you find your room too lonely after sharing a bed with a man?'

She flushed painfully, then went white. 'You—you told me this was the bathroom,' she stammered.

He put his hand on her left arm and she jerked away from him.

'I said turn left, Fay,' he reminded her sardonically. 'You've lost your sense of direction.'

She gritted her teeth. Had she done that? She lifted her eyes to his face, angry at the scepticism she saw there, and suddenly Dain pulled her towards him, like a dancer persuading a reluctant partner into his arms. Her toothbrush, her towel, her pyjamas flew in all directions, and she was held closely against him. She gasped as the softness of her satin-covered bosom slid against the bare skin of his chest. Before she knew it, he had pulled the top of her gown open and brought her naked breast into contact with his own hot skin—found her mouth with his own and was kissing her deeply, exploring, demanding. It was all so completely unexpected it simply took her breath away. It just—happened and—oh God, it was like falling into a heated pool in the darkness of night—overpoweringly sensual. Fay was utterly confused, utterly lost. Utterly unresisting. For a long moment she leaned against him helplessly, opening her mouth to him and aware of the prickling of her nerves.

Afterwards she was sure it was because she was so much taken by surprise and so wrung out that she gave in to him as she did, but when he murmured against her hair, 'Do you want to spend the night in my bed?' she came to her senses.

'No! *No!* Let me go at once or I'll scream the house down!' She struggled away from him frantically, pulling the edges of her robe together, her cheeks hectic, her pulses racing. Then she stopped to gather up her scattered belongings from the dark green carpet that gave his bedroom, with its tan and gold striped wallpaper and the big pots of ferns at the french doors, the look of a clearing in the jungle. A jungle in which he was the predatory beast, she thought, with frightened fancifulness.

'Who do you think would hear your screams?' he wanted to know, and she straightened up quickly, her eyes wide with fright. Then as she looked into his dark face and the glitter of his eyes, the room began to spin. She reeled and would have fallen if he hadn't caught her. She felt the blood drain from her face, her skin grow clammy. The room blurred and grew dark . . .

When her senses cleared, she was lying flat on her back on Dain's bed and he was stooping over her, a small glass in his hand. She caught the whiff of brandy as he raised her head with the other hand and put the glass to her lips.

'Here, get some of this into you.' His voice was rough—impatient, she thought. She sipped and gulped, her eyes riveted on his naked chest, with its mat of dark curling hair. She pushed the glass away, spilling some of the brandy on her bare skin, and with a gasp that was half a sob she covered her breast and struggled to sit up on the big double bed, only to have her head swim. Moaning, she lay back again, one hand covering her eyes.

'Just don't rush it,' he said softly, smoothing the feathery hair back from her brow. 'Do you often do this? Is it a—regular occurrence?'

She turned her face away from him, embarrassed. 'I'm—tired, that's all. Let me—let me go back to my room.'

'In a minute or two.' His voice was so close she could feel his breath warm on her face. 'Just give your body time to start working properly again. You haven't been eating, I suppose—you didn't eat enough for a bird at Mittagong. I'll make you an egg flip.'

'It doesn't matter,' she protested. 'I don't want anything—only to——'

'Shut up,' he said tersely. 'You'll do as I say. You'll stay where you are till I get you that egg flip, then I'm going to watch you get it down. I'll help you back to your own room—your own bed—when I'm satisfied you're ready for it. If you start staggering around now you're only going to fall over.'

He moved away and she opened her eyes and raised herself on her elbow to look around the room. It was very masculine and overpoweringly impregnated with his personality. Disconcertingly, a big mirror on the wall opposite showed her herself—pale and helpless-looking, in the middle of Dain Legend's vast bed which was covered with a quilted cotton cover in black, tan and avocado green. Rapidly, she slid her feet to the floor. She felt slightly nauseated, but the faintness had passed. Cautiously she stood up, found her towel and pyjamas but not her toothbrush, and, her legs shaking, her heart beating too fast, crept to the hall and made her way back to her bedroom.

There was no lock on the door and she stared about her with dismay, then with sudden inspiration fled to the hall again, this time turned left, found the bathroom, and bolted the door.

She had slipped off her robe and had the shower running when Dain tried the handle.

'You can't come in,' she shouted. 'I'm just getting under the shower.'

'Unbolt that door!' he shouted back, his voice angry. 'If you collapse in there with the door locked how the hell do you think I'm going to get in to you?'

'I won't collapse,' she muttered, but apart from that she paid no attention to him. She stepped under the shower and pulled the white and yellow nylon curtain across.

When at last she emerged from the bathroom he was waiting for her, and she saw at once that he had pulled on a pair of trousers over his shorts. His eyes ran over her quickly, her damp hair, her pale face, her shadowed eyes.

'I've put that egg flip on the table by your bed. Are

FIRST PASSION

you going to drink it, or shall I have to come and hold your nose?'

'I'll drink it,' she said, her voice low. She edged past him, ready to run if he should make a grab at her, though where she would run to she had no idea, and when Dain touched her arm she let out a frightened sob.

'What's the matter now?' he demanded roughly, and she looked at him, her eyes brimming with tears.

'I—I want to go home.'

Something in his face changed subtly and he leaned back against the wall and folded his arms. 'I'm afraid you're not going home, Fay. But calm down. Don't get the idea I brought you here to seduce you.'

'How can I help it?' she interrupted. 'And—and don't pretend you didn't—say what you did.'

'You mean I invited you to my bed?' His eyebrows rose. 'Well, you asked for it. You shouldn't have come to my room. That appears to be a bad habit of yours, doesn't it? Making somewhat inexplicable mistakes of that sort, late at night. And let's face it, you were very compliant in my arms. I can hardly be blamed for thinking you were willing to let me make love to you.' His eyes flicked over her thoughtfully, then came back to her face. 'Now we've both cooled down, we can forget it ... Drink up your egg flip, won't you? You'd better sleep in tomorrow. I'll have Mrs Lindsay, my housekeeper, bring you some breakfast in bed,' he concluded mockingly.

'Thank you.' Fay felt too limp, too drained to say any more, and once he had disappeared into his bedroom, she went into hers. She closed the door, dragged a chair against it, picked up the long glass containing the egg flip, and sat down on the side of her bed. She was trembling so badly she had to clutch the glass with both hands to raise it to her lips. Dain must have put a good slug of brandy in it, because once she was in bed with the light out, she drifted quickly into sleep.

In the morning when she woke, the sun was shining and the room looked very pretty with its yellow curtains and off-white walls, and its pale green floor rug. Her eyes moved to the chair under the door handle and she slipped out of bed and moved it away. She was none too soon, for a only a few minutes later someone knocked on the door, and woman's voice enquired pleasantly, 'May I come in?'

It was the housekeeper, Mrs Lindsay, a comfortable-looking woman of fifty or so. She wore a pale blue overall and white shoes, her brown hair was lightly streaked with grey, and her face was plump and soft and slightly freckled. The tray she was carrying was laden with fruit juice, toast, eggs and a pot of tea, and as she put it down on a small table near the bed she positively beamed at Fay.

'Did you sleep well, Miss Douglas? I hope you have a good appetite this morning!'

'It looks delicious,' said Fay, propping herself up on her pillows. 'Thank you very much.'

'No trouble,' Mrs Lindsay said, and after seeing that Fay was satisfied, she went out, closing the door behind her.

What had *he* told her? Fay wondered. She was hungry this morning, and as she ate she found she had practically forgotten yesterday morning and her discovery that Tony had walked out on her, taking most of her money with him. Her mind was more occupied with last night and Dain Legend. If she hadn't passed out, who knew what might have happened? She was positive she couldn't stay here with him—not on her own. And it didn't seem as if the housekeeper slept in. She almost wished Sondra were here—she'd make sure that Dain Legend and Fay Douglas were kept safely apart.

She almost wished it—but, curiously, not quite. Because honestly, she couldn't stand Sondra.

Dain was nowhere around when she emerged from her room and took her tray out to the kitchen, which she found at the back of the house. Mrs Lindsay told her in a friendly way, 'Mr Legend's gone out to the Old Woolshed paddock to see a buyer who's come to look at the wether lambs. He'll probably be out all day, he said. He didn't want to disturb you.'

Great, Fay thought. The less she saw of him the better she liked it. She dressed, taking her time, then wandered into the garden, crossing the wide gravelled circular drive to the parklike grass shaded by ancient pine trees. Because of the description she had read in the history Dain was writing, it all seemed a little familiar. She could see there had been money spent on both the old house and the garden, they were in such superb order, and there was a gardener at work in the grounds now. She stood in the shade of a huge purple-flowered bougainvillea looking back at the long low L-shaped house, its simple and elegant verandah draped with wistaria. Much as she admired it, she felt she couldn't possibly stay here until her mother and Walter came home. It would be months! She simply had to get back to Canberra and find herself another job. What did Dain think she was, that she could fritter her time away doing a little typing for him? The answer to that question was plain enough. Like Tony Thorpe, he saw her as the stepdaughter of a very wealthy man. There was no need for Fay Douglas to work!

She began to fume inwardly. She valued her independence—and it was a fact that her becoming Walter's stepdaughter had led to all this—to her losing her job, meeting Tony, coming here. 'I'll talk to him about it,' she promised herself, walking on beneath the trees and then pausing to look down over the rich pasture lands that sloped down to the river. She could see sheep grazing in one of the far paddocks, and across the river, hazy in the summer heat, she saw a group of buildings—cottages, stables, the big shearing shed, quarters for the men. Away beyond was the jagged line of mountains etched against a blue sky. It was all very beautiful, and she thought it was no wonder Dain loved the place, a fact that had been evident from the way he wrote of it.

Strolling on, she tried to imagine herself reasoning with him tonight, explaining that she really had to have a job—that she couldn't stay on here. But the sensible dialogue she tried to construct kept breaking off as she saw again those enigmatic black eyes, and felt the jolt through her body as he pulled her to him and kissed her.

She went back to the house. She would have to find something to keep herself occupied.

It wasn't difficult. Drifting into the big sitting room, she found propped up on a small table a message for herself. 'Fay, I suggest you use the breakfast room as your study. You'll find some work waiting for you there, and a typewriter. D.L.'

She spent most of what was left of the day typing.

At five o'clock she had had enough. It was time to stop—to shower and dress for dinner—with him.

He didn't come back alone. He brought the buyer with him—a stocky middle-aged countryman whose interests seemed to be sheep and beer and sheep again. The two men had a few drinks on the verandah before dinner, and when Fay joined them Dain introduced her offhandedly as 'My ward, Fay Douglas,' and then proceeded to ignore her. The buyer, Eric Lester, stayed for dinner and for the night. No concessions were made to Fay, the conversation was strictly sheep, the need for rain, the prospects for the year. Fay felt decidedly de trop. Though with her mother's friends she had always been satisfied to remain in the background, somehow it was different now. It was as if she had been a schoolgirl then, and now was an adult. Yet there was that feeling in the air that she should disappear, and finally she did. What was the use of staying, after all? Obviously she wasn't going to be able to discuss her own problems with Dain.

She was too wide awake, too restless to go to bed, but with a murmured excuse she went into the garden and walked about under the dark pines. The moon hadn't risen yet, but down in the valley across the river she could see the lights from the cottages. Mrs Lindsay lived over there, also Dain's manager, she had discovered. There must be a bridge and she wondered if she could find it, and followed faint wheel tracks that were difficult to pick up by starlight. But it was a long way—further than she had imagined—and the going was rough, and after some time she turned back towards the homestead again. The moon had risen now, and as she reached the gate that led into the courtyard behind the house she saw a dark shadow moving, and realised with a leap of the heart that it must be Dain—looking for her.

CHAPTER SEVEN

'I wondered where you'd got to,' said Dain as he drew near.

'Did you?' She asked it ironically. 'I hardly thought you'd noticed I wasn't there.'

They were in the shadow of one of the big pines and moonlight lay in silver streaks on his face and hair, while his eyes were dark shadows.

'I noticed all right,' he said dryly. 'I hope you weren't expecting me to come after you.'

'I wasn't—and I didn't want you to either,' she broke in.

'You weren't feeling neglected?'

She shrugged. 'I prefer my own company to yours, Mr Legend. Don't forget it was your idea I should come here, not mine. And that you practically blackmailed me into it.'

'Don't worry—I won't forget.'

Close to him like this she remembered last night with a vividness that was uncomfortable. Earlier, with Eric Lester making a threesome in the house, she had felt aloof and uninvolved and safe, but now the other thing came flooding back, and uneasily she moved away from him and turned towards the gate.

'Hang on,' he said, his hand on her bare arm. A current ran through her veins and she drew away from him instinctively.

'What do you want?'

'Nothing more than to ask how you got on today,' he said, and she could see from the slight curling of his mouth that he thought she had expected something quite different.

'I got on all right—since you weren't around,' she said with deliberate rudeness.

'Good. I thought you'd need something to distract you.' He had moved close to her again and taken cigarettes from his pocket. 'I imagined a little work might take your mind temporarily off your abortive love affair.'

'Did you?' Fay said jerkily. It was amazing how little she had thought of Tony and of those few days they had spent together. It was as though he had vanished almost without a trace, even though he had got off with all her money. True, she still had her two hundred dollars, because Dain had refused to take it and had settled the hotel bill from his own pocket. That had irked her somewhat because it put her in his debt, and that she didn't like.

'Work is supposed to be the panacea for all pain,' he remarked, and she said smartly,

'Then the longer I stay here the more work I'm going to need to do. Because I really find you a—pain in the neck, Mr Legend,' she finished deliberately.

There was a brief silence. Then, 'I don't care to have my ward speak to me like that,' he said coldly. 'You'll watch it in future, Miss Fay Douglas.'

Her cheeks had flushed and she felt a little thrill of excitement run along her nerves. 'I don't see how you can stop me saying what I like. You might be able to force me to stay here, but you can't gag me. And if I chose, I could tell tales about you, couldn't I?'

His hand shot out and imprisoned her wrist and he all but jerked her off her feet as he pulled her towards him angrily. 'You're a little bitch, Fay Douglas,' he bit out. 'I assure you if it weren't for the promise I made your mother I wouldn't let you even set foot on my property!'

'If my mother knew how little she could trust you she'd never have asked you for any promise,' she countered quickly.

'No? I'm beginning to think your mother knew damned well what she was doing.'

'What do you mean by that?' she flared.

'I mean she was well aware of your latent promiscuity—and possibly had hopes of palming you off on me before it all came out in the open.'

Fay uttered an exclamation of incredulity—and yet in her heart she knew there was a grain of truth in what he had said. Not as regards her promiscuity, but about the other thing. Because Claire had actually said that Fay might give him back a little of his faith in women. How wrong she had been! He was as cynical about her as he was about anyone—possibly even more so.

'If you hadn't got yourself so involved with Tony Thorpe, who knows? You might have been throwing yourself at me,' he said.

'I don't have to throw myself at you,' she retorted. 'You—you grab a handful of me just about every time we meet!'

Dain tossed down his cigarette and tramped on it, and she gasped as suddenly he caught her and crushed her against his body.

'You provocative little tramp!' His lips found her mouth and she felt the rasp of his chin against her tender skin as his kisses slid from her mouth to her neck and then to her bare shoulder. She heard the stitches rip as he pulled the narrow strap down, and she swallowed a sob that was half fear, half excitement.

'You—you brute!' She twisted her head and bit his ear—hard—then caught her breath as she heard his grunt of pain.

'That might teach you to leave me alone,' she panted.

'Come on—you know much better than that. My God, I've never known so innocent-looking a girl turn out so sexy. Come here——'

'Let me go,' she muttered. 'All I want is to—to get away from you——'

'Do you think I believe that? I know what you want——' The rest of his words were smothered against her mouth and she heard the soft hiss as he unzipped her dress down the back.

'Don't—don't!' Fay moaned helplessly as he slipped her dress off her shoulders. She wasn't bearing a bra and the moonlight dappled the whiteness of her breasts as he imprisoned her wrists with one hand while his eyes took their fill of her. Fay was filled with panic. This sort of thing had never happened to her before, and she had no idea how to escape. Last night she had fainted—largely through hunger and weariness. But tonight nature wasn't coming to her aid in any way. In fact, all her senses seemed to have come excruciatingly alive, and instead of struggling she let him draw her to him—kiss her mouth, kiss her naked breasts—while her heart beat dementedly and she felt the stirring of his body. They were locked in each other's arms, all her resistance was gone, all her self-respect. She slid one hand inside his shirt to feel his skin, while the other went to the back of his head to feel the thickness of his dark hair.

'Fix your dress up,' she heard him murmur a minute later. 'Let's get inside.'

She seemed to come out of a daze as Dain helped her hurriedly with her dress, and then he had thrust her ahead of him through the gate. Fay was shocked at her own behaviour as she stumbled through the garden towards the house. There were lights on the verandah and in the sitting room, and she wondered if Eric Lester had gone to bed and—exactly what Dain was expecting of her.

She knew soon enough, for in the warm dark of the hallway he whispered, 'I'm going into the bathroom for a minute. You go straight to my room——'

He left her, and for a paralysed moment she stayed where she was, listening to her heart beating, hearing her own hurried breathing. The clamour in her body had subsided—the passion he had invoked with his kisses, his caresses. She wasn't going to bed with Dain Legend, a man who had no respect for her, who thought she had already had a lover. She didn't want it, it was unthinkable. But what was she to do? His room lay to the left, her own room and the bathroom, from which she could see a slit of light shining under the door, were in the other direction. She had no idea where Eric Lester was sleeping, but in any case she could hardly run to him for protection.

'Men,' she thought wildly. 'I hate them!' Tony who had taken her money, Dain Legend who called himself her guardian and wanted to take her virginity—though that wasn't altogether fair, he thought she had lost that already.

Finally she did a crazy thing. She went quietly into her own bedroom, leaving the door a little ajar just as she had found it, and crawled under the bed.

She heard Dain emerge from the bathroom and pass her door and she stayed where she was, lying flat on her back. A moment later the door creaked faintly and he came into the room.

'Fay?' His voice was soft, and she didn't answer. She held her breath as he flicked the light on and then off again and went away. Stiff and uncomfortable, she stayed where she was and somehow she fell asleep.

At some unearthly hour she awoke and came out from her hiding place, hating herself just as much as, or even more than, she hated him. She went to the bathroom moving very quietly, then came back and got into bed, snuggling down into the unutterable comfort of its softness.

In the morning, Dain had gone out with the buyer before she was up. She looked a wreck, and Mrs Lindsay, seeing her haggard appearance, advised her to have an easy day—not to sit indoors working over the typewriter. Fay had made up her mind she was leaving. She was going to tell him so, and after that performance of last night he would surely release her.

She did no typing that morning. Her head ached and she was a mass of nerves and shame and hatred, her thoughts veering away every time they approached last night's encounter too closely. What a place to have come to be kept out of trouble! She sat on the verandah trying to distract herself by reading a book until Mrs Lindsay came to tell her that lunch was ready.

When she went into the dining room she was shocked to find he was there. He pulled out a chair for her and though he smiled at her, his eyes were hard and hostile. Fay sat down and thought that if she ate so much as a mouthful of food she would be sick, though the platter of cold meats and the two bowls of salad looked attractive enough.

'Help yourself,' said Dain, taking the seat opposite her. He wore moleskins and a black and tan checked shirt, and he looked horribly healthy and tough and very masculine. Fay was super-conscious of the mauvish shadows that lay like bruises around her own cornflower-blue eyes. If she had known he was going to be around she would have used make up to hide them—if she had come to lunch at all. She helped herself to a minimum amount of salad and a little ham and watched him numbly as he piled his own plate. When he had taken up his knife and fork he looked up and met her eyes across the table.

'What happened to you last night?' he asked bluntly.

She blushed scarlet and then paled as she hunted feverishly for something to say—something damning, something to put him in his place.

'Well, what made you change your mind?' He had taken a mouthful of food, masticated it and swallowed it before she answered.

'I didn't change my mind,' she said, licking the corner of her mouth nervously. 'I—I never intended to—to——'

'To come to bed with me? Who's talking about intentions, anyhow? We both got carried away, that's all. I didn't intend anything either, believe me, till you teased me into feeling that way. I must admit I enjoyed the game, but you were right not to play it to its conclusion. In fact, I'd reached the same decision myself, and even if I'd found you lying naked on my bed waiting for me, I was going to send you back to your room untouched—if I had to carry you there kicking.'

Fay swallowed a gasp. What sort of girl did he think she was? She burst out, 'You needn't have worried. I'd—I'd have to be dead before you found me on your bed, naked or otherwise!'

'Now don't take it that way,' he drawled, buttering another slice of bread. 'You're obviously very highly sexed, and that's just a thing we'll have to battle against together.'

Fay pushed back her chair. 'I thought I hated you before, Mr Legend, but—but now—I just hate you so much I could——'

'Oh, quit the amateur dramatics,' he said wearily, 'and let's be serious. You're your own worst enemy, Fay. Sit down and eat something, for heaven's sake. If we're going to live together we'll have to come to terms some way.'

She stood holding on to the back of her chair. 'We aren't going to live together! I want to go back to Canberra and find a job. I can't stay here.'

'And I can't keep an eye on you while you're in Canberra,' he said. 'I know only too well how little you're to be trusted. You told me I'd blackmailed you into coming here. Well, nothing's changed. You're going to stay put. I'm awake to the dangers now. Nothing happened last night and nothing's going to happen. I'll watch it, even if you don't.'

So nothing had happened, she thought. That was how he saw it. For her, a whole lot had happened—a whole lot of things that had never happened to her before. And though he talked about it as if it had all been her fault—teasing him, he'd said—what about the things he'd done? Pulling her clothes off her, all but seducing her. And yet he still thought of himself as her guardian! It was ludicrous. She couldn't have him telling Claire about her adventure with Tony. She was the only one who really knew what had happened and it suddenly occurred to her that she could write to her mother—get in first. That way, he couldn't possibly blackmail her. Then, she could tell Dain Legend to go to hell, and she could go back to Canberra.

'All right, I'll stay,' she said after a moment, and she saw she'd surprised him. 'But you'd better watch it—you're not the only one who can tell my mother—things.'

'Then sit down and eat your lunch and be civilised. You can come round the paddocks with me this afternoon, and it might be an idea if we drive over to the cottage and see if Sondra's there. She's your stepsister now and while I'm aware you aren't the best of friends, you should get to know each other better. I'll ask her to stay a few days and keep you company.'

Fay didn't protest. It was an unpalatable idea, but Sondra wouldn't leave her alone with Dain for a single second, and that was highly desirable. If he wanted to play games, he could play them with Sondra, she reflected. She was sure Sondra would be willing.

They drove through a couple of the big paddocks before they went to the cottage after first crossing the creek, not by a bridge but by splashing through the shallow water.

'A hundred years ago this river was alive with platypus and cod,' Dain remarked, regret plain in his voice, as they drove up the bank and through the willows on the far side, emerging near the buildings she had seen from the garden. It was a beautiful property, though very dry just now with summer nearing its end, and Fay was aware of Dain's pride in the place as he showed her the big shearing shed with its ten stands, the vast machinery shed, and the very modern stables. They had about sixty horses on the property, he told her, and a number of kelpies for working the sheep.

Later, he stopped to talk to a couple of his men who were shifting a mob of sheep to another paddock for fresh feed. Fay relaxed, and as they drove on she asked him curiously, 'Were those Marshalls who were here away back at the beginning any relation to Walter Marshall?'

'Yes. Your stepfather's a direct descendant,' he said. 'Sondra's cottage is one of the original buildings—a little house with two rooms and a verandah paved with handmade bricks—very attractive. Walter had it renovated for Sondra, and built a workroom and a kiln across the yard. The Marshalls retained only that and about twenty acres of land around it when they sold out and moved away ... Sondra's a very talented ceramic sculptor, by the way. I don't know if you're aware of that.'

Fay hadn't been aware of it, and somehow it made her feel nondescript and decidedly untalented.

'You'll probably see some of her work today,' Dain told her. 'She's never forgiven her ancestors for selling out, you know. That's why she clings to the cottage. But she won't stay isolated there too long—she's a very attractive girl.'

Listening to him praise her stepsister, Fay felt an odd spasm very like jealousy, but quelled it instantly. She wondered if he planned to be the one to put an end to Sondra's isolation.

'I've had dreams of sons taking over from me,' he continued a little bitterly. 'But so far I've been unlucky. My wife didn't want children.'

Fay glanced at him through her lashes. He had never spoken to her of his wife before.

'You're—divorced, aren't you?' she asked hesitantly. 'She—your wife—didn't marry again?'

'No,' he said briefly, curtly, and his eyes were veiled suddenly. If she had hoped to learn something about his marriage, she was disappointed, for he said no more on the subject and she didn't dare reopen it again—though why it should be of much interest to her she didn't really know.

They crossed the meandering creek again, then followed a fence and went through a gate, and after that it was only minutes before Sondra's cottage came into sight, as they rounded a curve of the long low hills.

Sondra was home and looking very attractive in a pale beige boiler suit worn over a green shirt. Her greeting to Dain was effusive, though she barely managed to speak to Fay at all.

'I gather you managed to run the juvenile delinquent to earth,' she remarked as they went on to the verandah. 'And she wasn't on her way to Paris after all.' She turned to Fay with a hard smile. 'You had everyone running round in circles looking for you, Fay. Hardly considerate of you, under the circumstances, was it?'

'I didn't think everyone was running round in circles,' Fay couldn't resist saying. 'Surely you weren't, Sondra!'

The other girl's blue-green eyes narrowed with dislike and she turned away and addressed Dain. 'Do sit down and I'll get some beer. I'm right in the middle of some work, as you might guess from my get-up, but I need a break.'

They all moved along the narrow brick-paved verandah in the direction of some outdoor chairs, and Dain waited till Fay was seated before he too took a chair. Sondra vanished inside—though not very willingly, Fay thought, and Dain remarked, his dark eyes sardonic, 'You're a beer drinker too, are you, Fay?'

She flushed. 'No, I don't care for beer.'

'Then why didn't you say so? You'd better go in and ask Sondra to get you a lemonade.'

Fay got up at once, smoothing down her fine blue denim skirt and feeling annoyed. She supposed she would have drunk the beer, but if Dain was going to make a thing of it then she would ask for something innocuous. She went through the house to the small kitchen where Sondra, with a scowl on her face, was putting glasses and some iced cans of beer on a tray.

'What do you want?' she snapped unwelcomingly.

'Could I have a soft drink of some sort, Sondra? I don't really care for beer.'

Sondra gestured towards the refrigerator. 'Help yourself.'

Fay was aware of being watched as she found a bottle of mineral water, and closed the fridge door. Her stepsister said nastily, 'Why have you come out to Legend's Run? I suppose you're planning to make a set at Dain now your affair with Tony's fallen through.'

'Not actually,' said Fay, forcing herself to sound unmoved.

The other girl glared at her. 'The more I see of you the less I like you,' she remarked. 'Why don't you stay in Canberra and keep out of the way? I've told you what I want—and you know what Dain thinks of you. You've got a free apartment and I wish you'd occupy it.'

Fay raised her eyebrows. 'You told me you'd look after it, Sondra,' she said sweetly as she made for the door. Sondra followed with the tray.

Fay drank her mineral water while the others opened cans of beer, and Dain took a long thirsty draught from his glass before remarking, 'So you're up to your neck in work, Sondra.'

'Yes. I've been working on a little group of cats—Siamese—for a man who admires my pieces. It's for his sister and I've rather rashly promised to have it ready in time for her birthday. Right at this minute I'm starting on a second set, just in case something goes wrong with the particular glaze I'm using. It's inclined to be temperamental and I particularly want to produce a good piece of work. Heaven knows, I'm charging enough,' she finished, laughing attractively.

'Well, I wish you luck,' said Dain. He finished his beer and set down his glass. 'Under the circumstances, we won't make demands on your time.'

Sondra's eyes sharpened, and Fay knew she hadn't liked that phrase, '*We* won't make demands on your time.'

'What do you mean, Dain?' she asked.

He shrugged his broad shoulders. 'Fay's staying at Legend's Run for a while. It occurred to me you could be company for her, but we'll forget it.'

Fay wanted to laugh at the look on Sondra's face.

Shock, fury and helplessness, all were combined very unhappily just for a second before she controlled her features. Very obviously there was little she could say since she had emphasised the fact that she was busy, but she found something. 'I'll drive over as soon as I have a spare minute. It's too bad if Fay is bored in the country.'

Dain nodded and smiled faintly. 'Don't interrupt your work. It's not important enough for that.' He stood up as he spoke. 'We'll get out of your way now and let you go back to your workroom.'

Fay had recovered from her slight amusement by now and was back with the unnerving prospect of continuing to be alone with Dain—at night. She thought of the letter she had determined to write and before going out to the car with Dain she asked her stepsister, 'Has there been a letter for me at the flat from my mother since I've—er—been away, Sondra?'

'Not that I'm aware,' was the chilly answer, and Fay bit her lip.

'I was hoping to have an address to write to. Do you have one, Sondra?'

'Not till I hear from my father. What's so urgent? I suppose you're in need of another handout since you left your job so casually.' She smiled brightly as she said it, but her eyes were venomous. Fay was aware of it even if Dain wasn't, and she retorted,

'As a matter of fact, I don't need another handout, Sondra. I'm being well looked after at Legend's Run.'

Oh dear, she thought, the minute it was out. She'd be made to pay for that little crack!

As they drove back to the homestead, Dain asked her unexpectedly, 'What's happened to the money Walter left for you, Fay?'

She turned her head away from him. 'What do you mean, what's happened to it?'

'Oh, come on,' he said irritably. 'You know what I'm asking. Do you still have it?'

'If I did,' she said coldly, 'would I have let you pay that hotel bill?'

He uttered an exclamation of disgust. 'There's no end to your gullibility, is there? You mean you handed over the lot to a con man—an adventurer——'

'No, I don't mean that at all,' she retorted with spirit. 'Much as it pleases you to think the worst of me, I used it to settle an account.'

'What account?' he asked sceptically.

'For some furniture. The things Walter put in the flat for my mother—and me.'

He laughed mirthlessly. 'Forgive me, darling, but that's not true. Sondra paid that account. She discussed it with me.'

'Sondra did not pay it!' Fay exclaimed furiously. 'And—and don't call me darling—and don't ask me to forgive you either. I've said I paid the bill and I did whatever Sondra discussed with you or—or told you. She's——' She stopped dead suddenly. She wasn't going to say what she thought about Sondra. It wouldn't make any difference to what Dain Legend believed. But now she was glad Sondra wasn't coming to stay. Her presence might have made Fay safe in one way, but on the other hand she was infuriating enough to make anyone have an apoplectic *fit* . . .

That night after dinner Dain disappeared to his office to work on his book. Fay sat alone in the sitting room. It seemed safer than going to her bedroom. She listened to the radio and looked through some of the books in a tall cedar bookcase that was built into the wall. In a volume of poetry by Lord Byron, her eye was caught by some lines in 'Don Juan': 'In her first passion, woman loves her lover. In all the others, all she loves is love.'

First passion. She shivered and read it again, remembering last night and how completely she had lost her senses out there in the moonlight. She closed her eyes a moment against a recollection that was painful. How could she have let such a thing happen? How could she have been roused to passion, for the first time in her life, and so easily—by such a man as Dain Legend? It was both incredible and unacceptable. 'In her first passion woman loves her lover——' Well, she didn't love Dain Legend—on the contrary. And he wasn't her lover and never would be, not while she had breath to fight him. She was ashamed and amazed that she hadn't fought him last night but had submitted so easily and so completely. It must have been because it was all so new to her—because she hadn't known where it was leading. Her excuses didn't really convince her, but she knew that next time it would be different.

Next time?

She replaced the thick volume on the shelf and turned back into the room, almost as if she expected to find him there behind her. But the room was empty and she returned restlessly to her chair and the radio. She felt lonely and moody. Where was Dain? Was he really working on his book? Or was he—keeping away, *watching* it? Taking care she didn't have another opportunity to—to tease him into—wanting her...

CHAPTER EIGHT

SONDRA turned up at the homestead the next afternoon.

Fay hadn't seen Dain all day. She had been typing further pages of his manuscript, but by four o'clock she had had enough, and she was in the garden when Sondra drove up. Out of politeness, she crossed the lawn and went to meet her. She had been watching some birds in the pine trees—a pair of mopokes sleeping on a branch close to each other—but now she left them. There was no one but herself to welcome Sondra, as Mrs Lindsay had gone home to her own cottage. She had been feeling bilious and headachey, so Fay had offered to see to dinner that night, and in fact she had been intending to go inside and see about the meal at any minute, before she showered and changed for dinner.

Sondra wore a soft straw hat that gave her an air of casual sophistication and she was smoking a cigarette in a long holder. Her blonde hair hung down silkily and she was dressed in a pale mole-coloured silk skirt and matching low-necked blouse. She gave Fay the most cursory of nods and without waiting for an invitation strode on to the verandah and settled down on the sofa there.

'Would you like some tea or a cold drink?' Fay asked politely.

'I'll wait till Dain comes in,' was the abrupt reply. 'Sit down. I want to talk to you.'

After a moment, Fay sat down on the other end of the couch, while Sondra looked her over thoroughly and insultingly, taking in her slightly soiled white jeans and high-necked black cotton skivvy. Then her stepsister drew on her cigarette and remarked, 'I ran into Dain on my way over here. We were talking about you.'

Fay's pulses gave a little jump and her heart sank. When Sondra talked to Dain about her, she was all too apt to tell him things that weren't true. She asked resignedly, 'What did you tell him this time, Sondra?'

The other girl shot her a poisonous glance. 'I didn't tell him anything. But he told me one or two things.'

'About me being such a pain in the neck?' Fay suggested, her colour rising.

'No. We're both quite clear on that. He told me he'd more or less had to bring you back here because he'd told your mother he'd see you didn't get into too much trouble. Though it's a bit late for that, isn't it?'

'Is it?' said Fay, her spine prickling. 'What do you know about it, Sondra?'

Sondra blew smoke, her grey-green eyes malicious. 'I happen to know something about Tony Thorpe, Fay ... Dain is pretty disgusted with you, sleeping around at your age as soon as there's no one there to keep tabs on you. *That's* why you're here, make no mistake about it. It's not because he wants you around, though I daresay you have other ideas, since you've found out about the run-down state of Confetti Downs.'

'If you've quite finished, Sondra,' said Fay when she paused for breath, 'there's something I'd like to say for myself, and that's that I haven't been sleeping around. I don't know what experience *you* had with Tony, but *I* certainly didn't sleep with him.'

'No? I know what you got up to in my father's apartment.'

'What did I get up to?' Fay asked angrily. 'I haven't the least idea what you're talking about.'

'Haven't you? Well, Dain knows Tony spent the

night with you there more than once.'

'How could he know, when I didn't do any such thing?' Fay exclaimed indignantly. 'Dain can't possibly believe that!'

'Oh, but he does.' Sondra leaned back, crossed her elegant legs and tapped ash on to the polished floor. 'I mentioned it to him—just to make quite sure he knows what you're like, my dear stepsister. So however hard you've tried to persuade him of your innocence you're not going to manage it—I've made sure of that.' She looked at Fay through her mascaraed lashes. 'When I really want something, I usually get it, so forget any idea you have of getting the better of me. You're not going to score a single point. I want Dain and I want Legend's Run, and if you get in my way I'll trample on you—with hobnailed boots if necessary,' she finished, surveying one elegantly shod foot.

'It's not necessary,' Fay said shortly. 'I don't want him or anything that goes with him. But I'm not going to put up with all the untruths you tell him about me. I'll—I'll tell him straight out you've been lying.'

Sondra smiled coldly. 'If it's a matter of choosing which one of us he believes, he's not likely to come down on your side, Fay ... What happened in Sydney, by the way? Did Dain have to boot Tony out?'

'I thought he'd have told you all about it,' said Fay. 'Seeing you're so—close.'

'I didn't bother asking,' Sondra shrugged. 'I can more or less guess anyhow. It wouldn't be hard to tear you apart once you'd discovered he wasn't loaded after all—and he'd found out the same about you. You should really thank me for making you pay that bill, otherwise Tony would have got hold of that money.'

Her guess had more than a little of the truth in it, but Fay made no comment. She just had nothing to say to Sondra about the matter. All the same she couldn't resist saying, 'If Dain has such a low opinion of me as you say, I can't understand why you're worried about my being here.'

'I don't believe in taking risks,' Sondra explained. 'Men are inclined to lose their heads—to be sentimental about young and helpless-looking girls, even if they know very well they're not as innocent as they look.'

Fay stood up. 'Are you staying for dinner?'

'Yes. I've already been invited—by Dain.'

'I see. Then will you excuse me if I leave you? I have to prepare the vegetables and get the chicken ready.'

'*You*?' Sondra exclaimed, narrowing her eyes. 'My, oh, my—you are busy, trying to impress *someone*! You're not in charge here, so don't go putting on an act. I know very well Mrs Lindsay sees to the dinner.'

'Not tonight,' said Fay. 'She's not well. I offered to do the cooking and she's gone home.'

Sondra smiled disagreeably. 'How right I was about you! You're trying to edge your way in already.'

Fay walked away in disgust.

Her stepsister didn't follow her to the kitchen, and there she took the chicken from the refrigerator and quickly composed a menu—Hawaiian chicken with baked bananas, jacket potatoes and green peas. Something that wouldn't fuss her. She had cooked often enough for her mother's visitors, and though the kitchen was unfamiliar she would have no problems. Once she had got things under way, she decided to forget about Sondra, and going to her room she deliberately chose a provocative dress to wear. Claire had given it to her for Christmas and she had worn it only once, finding it too sophisticated for her. It was a clear tangerine colour with a very low neck, and she was well aware that it would add to her years. She took a long leisurely shower and washed her hair. The dinner was in the oven and all she would have to do before serving it up was to cook the peas and prepare a green salad. There was a fresh fruit salad for dessert and she could whip some cream to decorate it.

Dain was home by the time she was dressed, and when she floated on to the verandah in her finery both he and Sondra stared at her. She knew she was looking rather vampish, complete with eye-shadow and mascara, and that the vibrant colour of the dress emphasised the pale delicacy of her skin. Dain's eyes went unerringly to the low neck of the dress that revealed the curve of her breast, and Fay felt selfconscious as she told him, 'Mrs Lindsay's gone home with a splitting headache and a bilious attack—but I suppose Sondra's explained that to you. I've taken over in the kitchen.'

'Forget it,' said Dain. 'You're hardly dressed for the role of cook anyhow.' He got up from his chair and moved towards the door. 'Sondra's invited me to the cottage for dinner. With your small appetite you should be able to satisfy yourself with a scrambled egg or some cold meat.'

He disappeared inside the house, and Sondra smiled triumphantly. Fay fumed inwardly. How mean could you be! It seemed only too true she couldn't win a trick. Sondra had made her look very silly, and part of it at least had been her own fault—getting dressed up like this, imagining she could——

Well, what had she imagined? Had she been trying to score over Sondra, after insisting that she didn't want Dain or anything that went with him? And if that was true, then why was she so put out? She should be glad they were disappearing, that she wouldn't have to put up with their combined company for the evenings. But she wasn't glad. She had been looking forward to the evening in some curious way—particularly when she had seen herself in the mirror in this dress. Now she wanted to howl, particularly when Sondra said into her thoughts, 'You see, Fay Douglas, I meant what I said. I hope you're beginning to catch on how little you mean to Dain.'

Yes, Fay was catching on. She turned her back on Sondra and went inside. Out in the kitchen the dinner was cooking merrily, and she would be the only one there to eat it. She went not to the kitchen but to her bedroom, where she slammed the door shut—and immediately wished she hadn't—kicked off her high-heeled shoes, pulled the tangerine dress over her head and threw it on the bed. She was just about to throw herself after it when the door opened and Dain came in. She stared at him angrily, forgetful of the fact that she wore only a half-slip and a flimsy bra. He had evidently had a quick shower and was looking handsome in light pants and a cream shirt that he hadn't yet buttoned up.

'You're throwing a tantrum, are you?' he said, his voice and eyes hard. 'Running round the house slamming doors. What's the matter? Are you put out because you haven't been invited out for dinner?'

Her cheeks flushed and her eyes blazed at him. 'I wouldn't go to Sondra's for dinner if it was the only place in the world there was any food,' she stuttered. 'It would—it would choke me, to sit at the table with you and Sondra.'

His eyes glittering, he crossed the room and took her by the shoulders, shaking her. 'What's got into you, you little fiend?'

'Don't shake me!' she breathed, twisting away from him. 'What do you think's got into me? I—I've cooked a dinner for you and the next minute you calmly tell me you're eating out, that's all.'

'My God—women!' she heard him say under his breath. Then, 'I thought you'd be glad to have me out of your hair. Or do you——' He stopped and started again. 'All right, then have it your way. Get your dress back on and I'll tell Sondra we're eating here. Come on now.' He snatched up her dress from the bed and she backed away, suddenly conscious of how little she had on. She crossed her arms over her chest and he grabbed hold of her, the tangerine dress in one hand, and tried to force her arms down. 'Do as you're told—get dressed!'

They wrestled together. Fay was breathing fast, her eyes bright with unshed tears. 'Why don't you go away?' she exclaimed wildly. 'Leave me alone—go back to Sondra! I don't want——'

She said no more. Dain had grasped her face between his two hands and his mouth was hard on hers. She might have promised herself she would fight him while there was breath left in her body, but right now there *was* no breath left in her body. His mouth was relentlessly against her own, he was pressing her back against the wall and one of his hands was inside the waistband of her slip, hard against her bare flesh. With his body so intimately close to hers she was only too well aware of how he was feeling, and even though she hated him she could still feel the treacherous upsurge of passion weakening her limbs. She made a sudden effort, pushing at his chest with all her strength. There was another brief struggle and he let her go. She was shocked at the hot desire in his eyes, at the slow heaving of his chest—and shocked too when, without another word, he strode away and left her.

From the silence of her room she heard the two of them leave some minutes later. First one car started up, and then the other, then silence surged back into the house. Fay stooped and picked up her dress from the floor. She was shivering and the room was growing dark. The house seemed terribly empty. She sat on the edge of her bed feeling helpless and full of despair. Why had she acted so stupidly? Why had she slammed her door—made such a fuss? She had made a complete fool of herself, and Dain's opinion of her, low at any time, must be even lower now. As for her opinion of him—she had come to the conclusion long ago that he was a brute, and she hadn't changed her mind. Just because he took it for granted Tony had been her lover, he didn't seem to care how he treated her.

After some time she got up from the bed, switched on the light, and pulled on her robe. In the kitchen she found the chicken overcooked, the bananas black as coal and oozing out of their skins. She forced down a little food, then, when she had tidied the kitchen and cleared up all signs of the mess she had made of cooking dinner, she went into the garden—wandered there restlessly, her mind obsessed with the thought of Dain, alone with Sondra in her cottage.

She didn't hear him come home. In fact, she didn't know whether or not he even came back at all. He wasn't about in the morning, the kitchen was undisturbed, and Mrs Lindsay hadn't put in an appearance. Fay made herself some toast and tea, dressed, tidied her room and then went into the garden to cut some flowers, getting some comfort from their fresh colours and their subtle fragrances. Inside, she spent a long time arranging them, but somehow she couldn't become sufficiently engrossed to shut her mind off from Dain. Where had he spent the night? It was obvious, of course. His bed hadn't been slept in—unless he had remade it himself this morning. And she had thought that she could beat Sondra at her own game! Not because she wanted Dain Legend, of course, but because she objected to being treated as Sondra was treating her.

That afternoon she still didn't get back to the typing she was supposed to be doing. She sat on the verandah trying to make up her mind to walk down the paddock to the other side of the river and ask someone at the stables to saddle a horse for her so she could take a ride. But before she had gathered the energy to put her plan into action, Mrs Lindsay arrived and came through the house to let Fay know she was back. She didn't look at all a good colour, but she insisted she was fine.

'I'll see to a few things anyhow, dear—get something fixed up for your dinner and that. Mr Legend called in earlier on to ask how I was and to tell me to let you know he won't be in to dinner. He's going across to Breadalbane to see some rams and he might stay away the night. It's a shame you couldn't have gone with him.'

'Oh, it doesn't matter,' Fay said uncomfortably. She often wondered what Mrs Lindsay must think of her being here alone with Dain, and because of that she had been inclined to avoid talking to her. But now it seemed Mrs Lindsay was all ready for a talk and there was no way she could avoid it.

'You must be lonely here by yourself. I thought it might cheer you up if I came over for a little while. I won't bother you, Miss Douglas, but I know myself it's a comfort to know there's someone else around. Mr Legend should really get a housekeeper to live in.'

'Yes, it's a big house,' Fay agreed. 'I—er—I did some flower arrangements this morning, but you keep everything so beautifully clean that I didn't see much point in doing any housework.'

'Goodness gracious, you mustn't think you have to do that! You do like it here, don't you? I mean, it's not like the outback—it's close to Queanbeyan and Canberra. Women here have a very good life—the best of two worlds, I always say. You can even get over to the coast in a couple of hours if you feel like it. I have a married daughter at Bateman's Bay, but it's not so easy for me to get away with Mr Legend depending on me here and my own house across the river. Ah well, once he marries again he'll engage a full-time housekeeper, I'm sure.'

She was looking so hard at her that Fay felt the colour rise in her cheeks. Was the woman hinting that Dain might be planning to marry her, Fay Douglas, for heaven's sake? Just because she was staying here in this big house and—seeing how she liked it, presumably. She simply didn't know what to say, so she remarked with a nervous laugh, 'Perhaps he doesn't want to marry again.'

'Don't you believe it!' Mrs Lindsay said emphatically. 'Up to now it's understandable he should put it off, the worry he's had ever since he found his ex-wife was dying of leukaemia. I don't know what she'd have done without him. One shouldn't speak ill of the dead, but she didn't deserve it, running off with someone else as she did—who left her when he knew she was ill. Well, it's all over now and there's going to be changes ahead. I was as happy as could be when he brought you back here with him after you lost your job. It'll give you a chance to see how you like it at Legend's Run.'

Fay's face had gone crimson as she listened, and seeing it, Mrs Lindsay said ruefully, 'There, now I've embarrassed you. I apologise, but don't fret. With your sweet open face no one's going to get any wrong ideas about what's going on ... And now I'd best stop gossiping and do what I came to do.'

With a warm smile she vanished inside, and Fay sat thinking in some confusion of what she had said. One thing was clear, and that was that Dain's ex-wife had died of leukaemia, recently. That, she thought, appalled, was why he had gone to Melbourne—why he had had to break his appointment with her. Obviously he believed Sondra had explained to her and that she——

Oh God! How callous and selfish he must think her —at a time like that, to have been so wilfully making a nuisance of herself! How she wished now that she had never had anything to do with Tony Thorpe. She had proved herself quite irresponsible over that meaningless little affair—though it hadn't even been that. It had been—an ego trip, that was all. She had been idiotically and naïvely flattered because such a good-looking man had paid some attention to her.

Why hadn't Sondra explained to her? she wondered futilely; though she knew the answer to that question well enough. It suited Sondra that he should have a poor opinion of Fay Douglas. And he did. Mrs Lindsay was quite wrong to believe he wanted to marry Fay, now his worry about his first wife was over. If he married again, it would probably be Sondra. She had said she always got what she wanted, and with the methods she was prepared to use, it wasn't surprising. The thought filled her with a curious feeling she couldn't analyse. It wasn't as if she cared *who* he married. She didn't. Her basic feelings for him hadn't changed. She understood him a little better—felt sympathy for him, compunction at her own behaviour. But she still disliked him ...

That night she was alone again. Dain hadn't come back, but she didn't really think he was spending the night at Breadalbane. It was far more likely he was where he had been last night—at Sondra's. Well, who cared?

Dinner over, her dishes cleared away, she went into the sitting room and looked along the bookshelves for something pleasant to read. But it was no use; she couldn't settle to anything. Her mind was seething with a jumble of thoughts and images and emotions, and every one of them was connected with the man she disliked so much. She thought of what Mrs Lindsay had said about Dain getting a housekeeper to live in—how much more cheerful it was to have someone about the house. 'If I were married to him——' she thought, and at that point her thoughts stopped dead. She abandoned her efforts to read, allowed her tears to flow and went to bed.

And of course she couldn't sleep. She could think of nothing but the man who had invaded her life. Those dark eyes, that cruel mouth that had lain against her own so sensually. Lying restlessly awake in the dark, she heard herself groan aloud.

At that, she sat up and switched on the reading light. The way she was thinking about him now wasn't the way she was used to thinking about him. She groaned again. She wanted him to be here, in this house—she wanted to tell him she was sorry for a number of things—she wanted him to talk to her—— Instead, it was Sondra he was talking to. Oh, she was sure of it, agonisingly sure. Agonisingly? Yes—because she longed for him to be here with her. And not just—talking to her.

She left her bed distractedly and wandered through the French doors on to the verandah, feeling the polished boards cool and smooth under her bare feet.

'You're mad,' she told herself, leaning against the wall beside the doorway and looking hazily through the motionless vine leaves into the garden. She wanted to be in his arms again, her body afire with those passionate desires he roused in her so easily. The cool lawns traced with dark tree shadows stretched away emptily in the moonlight. She couldn't hear a sound, and she felt terribly small and alone and unimportant. How different it would be if she were married—living here with the man she loved. But he was with Sondra.

She blinked with shock at her own thoughts. The man she loved? Sudden tears rushed to her eyes. Yes, she thought defiantly, she loved him and she was jealous—sickeningly jealous—of Sondra. The moonwashed garden trembled as though it were afloat, and then distantly she heard the sound of a motor. It was Dain coming back! The world was suddenly a different place. She dried her tears quickly and soon car lights swept round the curve of the drive. Then silence again, darkness, the soft clunk as a car door was closed, and in moments he had come on to the verandah—and was striding towards her where she stood in shadow beside the strip of soft light that fell through her bedroom door.

Dain stopped inches from her and she felt her breast moving as her breathing quickened.

'Why aren't you in bed asleep?' He stood looking down at her and without meaning to she laid her hand on his arm as if she were in a dream. Dain Legend. The man she loved.

The stuff of his shirt was cool from the night air but the flesh beneath it was warm and she felt a shiver that was purely sensual run through her. She raised her face to his.

'I couldn't sleep,' she said huskily, then caught her breath as he took her roughly into his arms.

His mouth was on hers as he swept her up in his arms and carried her through the door into her bedroom.

She didn't fight him or even think of it this time. She lay on the bed where she had fallen with him half on top of her and felt the racing of her blood as his hand moved over one rounded breast, and the sickness of desire rose in her like a flood. It was she who unfastened the buttons of her pyjama jacket so that his hand could touch her skin, and she parted her lips to him as her body curved against his. Her mind was in a turmoil as she caressed the back of his neck with trembling fingers, and she longed to tell him how she had missed him, how jealous she had been, how much she loved him——

'Dain——' It was a half-whisper, a half-groan against the corner of his mouth, then they were kissing fiercely again, their bodies locked together. His lips moved to her breast and she was acutely aware that in a minute—it was going to happen. They were going to make love—nothing could stop either of them.

It was at exactly that point that something in her said *No*—as though a watchman who had fallen asleep had suddenly roused to danger. And in almost the same instant Dain raised his body from hers and swinging round sat on the side of the bed. To undress, she thought, her heart pounding with fright now as well as with passion. Because after all she couldn't—not like this, not until she had——

'Dain?' she said again, her voice husky, and he turned his head and looked down at her, his eyes black and hard, his mouth twisting.

'No, thanks, Fay Douglas,' he said thickly. 'I'm not going to accept your invitation.'

'My invitation?' she echoed blankly.

'Your appeal to my lust,' he said, dark brows descending over glittering eyes. 'You certainly had me all worked up, but I'm not all that interested in your cheap little body that you offer round so blatantly. I don't want the use of it, thanks. I've changed my mind.'

'Don't—don't say things like that to me, Dain Legend,' she gasped. 'I've never slept with Tony Thorpe—or with anyone else.'

'No?' His mouth curved cynically. 'I'd have to make love to you just once to prove how much truth there was in that statement, Fay.'

'Then make love to me,' something inside her wanted to cry, but she forced the words back. No more hysteria—she had to come to her senses. He had no tender feelings for her and she had been out of her mind—she must have been—to think she was in love with him. It probably had something to do with loneliness, with the antipathy she felt towards Sondra, that was all.

'You women,' he muttered with bitterness and contempt. 'Faithless and shallow and vain—lovely and poisonous and natural liars.'

'You have—preconceived ideas,' she said unsteadily. 'You—you can't say that kind of thing about all women. I—I might as well say——'

'You can say what you like,' he interrupted, getting to his feet. 'But don't ever again try to get me to go to bed with you.'

'I didn't!' she exclaimed, but his eyebrows rose sceptically.

'Weren't you waiting for me on the verandah just now? Well, goodnight. I'm going to my own room. I want some sleep.'

He slung off, and Fay snapped off the light with a fierce movement and got into bed, pulling the sheet up to her chin. Quivering, she could still feel the warmth from his body where he had been lying, and she stared wide-eyed into the darkness. Her heart felt bruised by his cruel remarks about her offering her body around, and by his pronouncing her, along with all women, a liar—and faithless. If he hadn't drawn away when he did, if he had gone ahead and made love to her, he would have discovered how wrong he had been, known that this was her first experience of sex.

The mad idea came into her head that she must prove to him that he was wrong, and before she knew it she was out of bed and half way along the hall to his room. Then suddenly she stopped dead in her tracks. She was mad. She couldn't do what she had planned—she just wasn't that kind of a girl. Even if she loved him, there was a limit to what she could do.

She must have uttered a sob, because Dain's door opened and he came into the hall, still fully dressed.

'What's the matter now? What the hell do you want?'

She flinched at the scorn in his voice. His opinion of her was so low it could go no lower. And she had contemplated offering herself to him to prove her virginity!

She said shakily, 'There was something I meant to say to you, Dain. I—Mrs Lindsay was talking to me today—and I—I realised you'd just lost your wife. I'm—sorry——'

'My ex-wife,' he interrupted harshly. 'But it can hardly have just sunk in when you were aware I had to go to Melbourne because Lois was dying. So don't use your pseudo-sympathy as an excuse for running after me again tonight.'

'I'm not using it as an excuse,' she burst out. 'And I didn't know a thing about it till today. But what's the use? You never believe a word I say. And I *am* sorry.'

His face was rock-hard. 'Save your sympathy. I don't need it. I've just given you an earful of my opinion of women in general and it still stands. Lois was a great girl, but she didn't know what loyalty is. Men found her attractive and she couldn't help herself. Then she discovered she was dying of leukaemia and that no one wanted her. One could say she reaped what she sowed, if one liked to point a moral. I loved her once—dementedly—but all that disappeared like grass in a drought. I'd still have brought her back to Legend's Run when she was ill, but she refused to come—and be alone with me.'

'I'm sorry,' Fay murmured, distressed. Though he spoke harshly she could see from the movement of a nerve in his jawline that he was affected by what he was saying. 'I wanted to tell you that I didn't understand when I went away with Tony and caused you such trouble. I'd have waited if I'd known, Dain.' Her eyes widened, imploring his belief.

'Would you?' he said coldly. 'I doubt if it would have made any difference.' His glance flickered over her as she stood barefoot in her crumpled yellow pyjamas, her face pale, her eyes shadowed. Then he turned away. 'Go back to your room, Fay, and for God's sake stay there. We're too much alone in this house. We'll have to give some thought to what's to be done with you.'

'Yes,' she agreed bleakly, her head bowed. He meant, of course, that she would have to go away, and even though she knew he was right, she couldn't greet the prospect with cries of joy. It was too late for that.

CHAPTER NINE

IT began raining in the early hours of the morning—hard heavy rain that sounded almost tropical on the iron roof of the homestead. It woke Fay from an uneasy sleep and she lay listening to it, but too troubled to enjoy the sound. All she could think of was that Dain was going to make some plan to be rid of her. And that what she wanted most of all was to stay here.

That this should have happened to her! she thought, shedding a few tears into her pillow. That she should be hungry for him—a man whom she had been quite sure she hated. So was it love—this obsessive feeling she had never had for Tony? She felt as if she had aged ten years in the last twenty-four hours.

When she got up in the morning it was still raining. The sky was black with clouds and the air was warm and sticky.

'My goodness, that rain!' Mrs Lindsay exclaimed when Fay went out to the kitchen to say she didn't want a big breakfast. Dain had gone and she felt both relieved and frustrated. 'What a good thing Mr Legend came home last night after all! I guess he heard the weather report. He generally starts shifting the sheep from the valley around this time, but they'll be at it from dawn till dark now—starting with Black Creek and Brumby's Flat. They're a man short too, with young Gary concussed from that fall he had, showing off the other day. Mr Legend will be late in tonight, I shouldn't wonder.'

'I guess he will,' Fay said slowly—as if she knew anything at all about it! She felt very much an outsider. She didn't suppose Dain would have any time today to think about what was to be done with her, anyhow. He had other far more important things on his mind, and she wished she knew enough to help with mustering the sheep. She would probably only get in the way, though. Sondra now, she thought wryly, she wouldn't get in the way. She might even be out in the paddocks with him now, filling in for 'young Gary'.

She worked at the typing that day. She had been neglecting it, and it was one thing she could do for him and it would keep her mind occupied. Dain came home long after dark. It was still raining and he looked haggard. He took his boots off on the verandah, went to the bathroom for a wash, then came straight in to the dining room for his meal. Mrs Lindsay had gone home hours ago. The creek was up, but there was a bridge some way downstream, and she didn't want to take the walk in the dark.

Dain ate his meal in silence, and barely glanced at Fay sitting opposite him in her long-sleeved voile blouse and black skirt. She felt a fool for dressing up since he was still in his working shirt and moleskins, his hair rough, his jaw and upper lip unshaven and dark. Dinner over, she stacked up the dishes and determined she would ask him some intelligent questions and put out a feeler in case there was some way she could help with the mustering. After all, she could ride.

But when she went inside he wasn't in the sitting room. Nor was he in his bedroom, for she could see through the open door that he wasn't in his bed. She wandered round the verandah, looking into the garden and wondering if he had gone over to Sondra's cottage, then accidentally she discovered him lying on a stretcher on the east verandah—deeply asleep and fully dressed except for his boots. With a feeling of helplessness, she fetched a cotton blanket from one of the other stretchers and draped it over him. He moved slightly but didn't wake, and Fay stood looking down at him, her eyes, accustomed to the darkness, taking in the darkness of his thick lashes, the black of his hair, the line of his mouth relaxed in sleep and devoid of its waking cynicism. He had a strong face, but now he looked utterly weary and defenceless and she had to fight against a strong desire to touch him. It would never do to wake him and find her there—inviting him. Quietly she tiptoed away.

The next day followed the pattern of the first, only the rain wasn't quite so thick. Mrs Lindsay arrived in an old car and left early after Fay insisted she could manage dinner. This time she didn't dress up but sat down to table in jeans and a plain shirt.

He ran his eyes over her as he ate his steak.

'You haven't dolled yourself up tonight. Did my failure to react last night disappoint you? I'm afraid I wasn't much in the mood for sexual stimulation—and in case you're wondering, I'm not tonight either.'

Fay clenched her teeth. She hadn't an idea how to deal with remarks like that. It was no use protesting that she hadn't dressed up for his benefit last night either, because in a way she had. Though it hadn't actually been with—sexual stimulation in mind! When she found nothing to say he went on conversationally, 'Don't imagine I don't appreciate you when you've made yourself look seductive. I assure you I do—you please my eye and my other senses inordinately. I'm even inclined to forget the serpent that's concealed by the loveliness—and you did allow that last night, didn't you? Is it embarrassing if I enquire if that was because you found me rather less appealing unshaved and in my working clothes?'

His eyes mocked her and his smile was inscrutable,

and she was goaded into saying, 'Since you mention it, I don't find you nice to be near.'

'I could soon make you change your mind,' he said with a narrow look.

She laid down her fork, her hand shaking. 'If that's a challenge, I don't want to accept it.'

'Why not, I wonder,' he said lazily. 'That treacherous body of yours? It's very highly inflammable, isn't it?'

Fay didn't answer him. Instead she asked, 'Are you managing to shift your sheep from the valley?'

He looked at her in some surprise as though he hadn't expected her to take any interest in station affairs. 'Sure, we've nearly got it beaten.'

'I was wondering if I could help in some way. I mean—I can ride,' she faltered, aware of his scepticism. 'So if there's anything I can do——'

'There's nothing,' he said shortly. 'I wouldn't dream of asking you to ride out after my sheep in the rain. Next thing you'd have pneumonia——'

'And I'm nuisance enough without that, aren't I?' she broke in bitterly.

'You could say that,' he agreed, pushing his plate aside. 'I've been thinking about the problem that came up the other night, by the way. I have one or two ideas.'

'What are they?'

He looked at her across the table. 'We'll go into it some other evening when I'm not so dead beat. You'll have to excuse me tonight—I have another long day ahead of me tomorrow. How have you been filling in your time? Longing for the bright lights?'

'No. I've nearly finished that typing for you,' she said, raising her eyes to his. 'That's why I thought perhaps I could go out with you tomorrow. There's not a lot to do with Mrs Lindsay coming in and I'd—I'd like to see a little more of Legend's Run. I've been interested reading your book.'

'Thank you,' he said ironically. 'That's one of the very few agreeable things you've ever said to me, Fay.'

She felt herself flush, but she was aware of a faint shock. 'You haven't been exactly pleasant to me either, Mr Legend.'

'No.' He got up from the table. 'With a little luck I may be in earlier tomorrow evening,' he said. 'In which case we'll discuss your future.'

As it happened, the sun was shining again next day, so Fay wouldn't have been in danger of catching pneumonia if she had gone out with him. But by the time she got up he had gone, and she sighed frustratedly. She spent the morning completing the typing she had to do for him and early after lunch she heard the sound of a motor and ran outside eagerly, thinking perhaps he had come back for her.

But it wasn't Dain; it was Sondra.

'What a welcome!' her stepsister said ironically as she came on to the verandah. 'Who did you think it was? I happen to know Dain's out mustering sheep. Or were you expecting Tony? I heard he was around again when I was in Canberra this morning—that woman at the florists said he'd been there looking for you.'

'Well, I haven't heard from him,' said Fay. She sat down and resigned herself to putting up with Sondra's company. She wondered fleetingly if perhaps Tony wanted to pay back the money he owed her, but strangely it didn't seem to matter much now. It would certainly be nice to have her savings returned, but she didn't want to see Tony.

'He'll probably be in touch with you,' Sondra said. 'He owes you some money, I believe.' She put a cigarette in her long holder and lit up, then asked, 'Isn't it about time you went back to the flat? I really can't look after it—I still have a lot of work to do out here. I made the trip in to Canberra especially to check that everything's all right, but really it can't go on, and when I saw Dain yesterday, we both agreed you'll have to go back to town.'

Fay's eyes opened wide. So Dain had been discussing her future with Sondra! She hated the thought.

'If we're going to marry, we want you out of the way,' Sondra continued brutally. 'And this morning I found a job for you. It seems you can't go back to Hearts and Flowers, but a friend of mine, an etcher who runs a little gallery in Manuka, is willing to take you on just as soon as you can come.'

'I don't know that I want to work in an art gallery, Sondra,' Fay protested, but the other girl broke in rudely,

'No one's asking what you want, Fay. I'm *telling* you you're going to take this job, and you'd better start packing. Right now. You can come to Canberra with me this afternoon and I'll introduce you to Samantha.'

'I'm not going today,' Fay said quietly but so firmly she surprised herself. 'Dain wants to talk to me tonight about my plans and I'm not going anywhere without discussing it with him first. I did that once—thanks to you—but I'm not doing it again. Before I go anywhere, I'll have his permission.'

Sondra's lips thinned and she tapped ash angrily on to the floor. 'All right, discuss it with him. But I'll be back for you tomorrow, and if you know what's good for you, you'll tell Dain you want the job, and you want to go. Do you understand? If not, you'll be sorry. I want you off Legend's Run. You're such a sneaky little bitch I wouldn't trust you as far as I can spit. You're to have your bags packed when I come tomorrow.'

Fay didn't answer. She didn't even say goodbye as Sondra got up and went out to her car.

What was she going to do? she wondered as the red car disappeared among the trees. She couldn't really believe Dain was going to marry Sondra, though it was true enough he wanted to be rid of her. Would he agree to let her go back to Canberra and take this job? Or would he still maintain he couldn't trust her out of his sight and perhaps palm her off on one of the families who worked on the property? There she would be safe enough and he could forget her for most of the time yet still check up on her until her mother and stepfather came back and took over.

Inside the house, she heard the telephone ringing and jumped to her feet and ran to answer it.

'Is that you, Fay? It's Tony here,' a male voice said, and her spirits sank. 'Look, I know you must feel like hanging up on me, but let me say something first—please!'

'What?' Fay asked flatly. That voice that had thrilled her so much didn't thrill her at all any more, nor did the image that the voice conjured up. He was far too good-looking—he had really taken her for a ride—and he had lied to her about his father's property too. 'I wonder you dare speak to me,' she heard herself say.

'I guess you do. And if you were here, Fay, I'd go down on my bended knees and ask you to forgive me. I behaved very badly and I admit it. But I did come back to look for you at the hotel the next day and found you gone, so there was nothing I could do.'

'What do you want?' Fay asked, cutting him short and not knowing whether or not to believe him.

'Most of all I want to see you again—and of course I'll pay you back that money you loaned me,' he said promptly. 'I can explain about that, Fay. The fact is, I fell for you really hard and I wanted to give you everything. But we've had a few bad seasons at Confetti Downs and my father refused to send me any money. That was the whole problem, because I'd made my plans in the belief I could splash it about and I was in a fix.'

Fay was sceptical. She wasn't nearly as gullible as she had been a short while ago. 'Then how are you going to pay me back?' she asked coolly.

'I rang home,' Tony told her. 'I told my old man the whole story and he's agreed to lend me the money—to take it out of my future pay. It's only fair. It's not all that much really. I managed to get some of it back from the travel agency. So listen—when can I see you?'

'I don't know,' she said cautiously.

'You're coming back to Canberra, aren't you? Mrs—er—the woman at the flower shop seemed to think you'd be back at the flat pretty soon.'

Did she? Fay was puzzled. But possibly Sondra had talked to Mrs Markham. As for whether she would be going back to Canberra, it really depended on Dain. She said hesitantly, 'I don't really know when I'll be coming back to Canberra, Tony. You'll have to ring me again—or perhaps I could get in touch with you,' she amended. 'Where are you staying?'

'The same motel as before—but only for another few days. So don't forget—make it as soon as you can.'

'I'll be in touch,' she said, and with a brief goodbye she hung up. She had very mixed feelings about the business. She didn't want to see Tony again, but naturally she wanted her money back—in which case she would have to see him soon, somehow or other.

She went out to the verandah again and in no time was worrying about the predicament Sondra had placed her in—threatening her with what? she wondered, if she didn't play ball and leave Legend's Run. It was easy enough to tell herself there was nothing Sondra could do if she didn't get her own way, but she had had experience of her stepsister before and knew she was quite unscrupulous. She had convinced Dain that Tony had stayed with her overnight at the flat, and that was only one of the mean vicious things she had done. She wanted Dain and Legend's Run and nothing was beyond her. Fay thought of the hobnailed boots and shivered.

When Dain came home, early as he had half promised, she had showered and was dressed for dinner, having compromised between formal and casual dress by wearing the black skirt and a simple off-white button-through blouse. She knew she was going to have to put Sondra's proposition to Dain, but she had a strong feeling that he wouldn't accept it, that he had ideas of his own. She attempted to bring the subject up for discussion over dinner, but he quashed it. He was looking devastatingly masculine in dark hip-hugging pants and a navy shirt. His jaw was freshly shaved, and as she caught the perfume of his after-shave she felt her pulses quicken.

'You said we'd talk about plans for my—my future tonight,' she said when their dinner was served and they were sitting down.

'Now?' he objected frowningly. 'Can't we have our dinner in peace first of all? Afterwards we can go into it.'

Damn! Fay thought rebelliously. She had screwed up her courage to say even as much as she had, and now she wasn't allowed to go any further. And it would be so safe to talk across the table—if talking to him could ever be safe—for her. Which she doubted, for she found it hard enough to keep her eyes off him, and presently he raised his own and caught her at it.

'What's the matter?' he asked half irritably, half quizzically. 'Is there something on your mind that you keep staring at me?'

'Only that I've fallen in love with you,' she thought, but aloud she uttered an embarrassed denial and forced herself to keep her attention on what she was eating.

Afterwards they took their coffee on to the verandah. The sky had clouded over again, and big clouds rushed across the darkness of the sky so that the bright stars showed through only fitfully. A mopoke called mournfully, and from across the river a dog barked, but otherwise it was as if they were alone in the world.

Dain said after a long silence, 'Well, we must talk about this business, I suppose. I told you I had one or two ideas, Fay——'

'Yes, but I have an idea of my own,' she interrupted nervously, and he looked at her with a frown.

'Well then, let's hear it.'

'I want to go back to Canberra to the flat,' she said abruptly. 'I can get a job in an etcher's gallery in Manuka.'

He leaned back in his chair and looked at her through narrowed eyes. 'How did you work this up, seeing you've been cooped up here every day? Have you been on the phone?'

'No, but Sondra mentioned it. The—the job, I mean. She was here today and she knows I want to start work again.'

'I see. So you've had enough of country life.'

She didn't look at him but at her hands that were nervously twisting together. 'What I've seen of it,' she said evasively.

'Which is precious little,' Dain remarked, and she waited, expecting him to offer her an alternative. But he didn't. He said, 'Well, I suppose I can't stop you. God knows I don't want to keep you here against your will. It's probably best you should go.'

His complete capitulation was unexpected and somehow it hurt. Before, he had been so concerned about—supervising her. Now it looked as if Sondra was going to win, hands down. Her stepsister must have been telling the truth after all—they must be thinking of marrying, and want her out of the way.

'So what do you propose to do?' he asked.

'Pack,' she said bleakly. 'I'll leave tomorrow.'

He was looking at her enigmatically. 'You've surprised me, Fay. I thought——' He stopped, and she looked at him through her lashes.

'What?' she prompted.

'Nothing.' He got up from his chair. 'Well, that's been settled quickly. Do you want to take a walk in the garden?'

'No,' she said, her voice low and quivering. 'I'll go and start my packing.'

'How are you getting to Canberra? I can't take you tomorrow, I've too many other things to do.'

'It doesn't matter. Sondra said she'd take me in her car.'

After that, Dain simply walked away. Fay watched him stroll across the grass and she stood up and hesitated. Of course she wanted to walk in the garden with him, but if she did, she knew what would happen—and she knew she would be blamed for it. Provoking him, teasing him, inviting him—womanlike. Before she could give way to a reckless impulse, she went inside to her room and opened her suitcases. She hated herself because she was doing exactly as Sondra had told her to do, and she hated Sondra. But perhaps she wouldn't take that job after all. She could get in touch with Tony and once she had some money to live on, she could take her time looking for work. She had a feeling anyhow that the job at the gallery wouldn't last, that it was a matter of her friend doing Sondra a favour.

She took off her shoes and without enthusiasm began arranging her clothes in neat little piles. She had thrown the wardrobe doors open, but the idea of folding her dresses was just too much tonight. There'd be plenty of time tomorrow. Sondra would simply have to wait, that was all. She wondered what she was going to say to Mrs Lindsay, who so romantically imagined she might marry Dain. But after all, she didn't have to tell her anything except that she was going back to Canberra.

She wandered across the room towards the verandah door, then uttered a little gasp. Dain was there, leaning against the doorframe, watching her. Their eyes met and a flame ran through her. She wanted to throw herself into his arms and beg him, 'Love me!' She kept walking towards him slowly, like a sleepwalker.

'How's the packing going?' he drawled as she stopped a foot away from him, her breathing fast, her head lowered.

'I'll—do it tomorrow,' she said on a breath, and he reached out and caught her to him.

'Why not?' he muttered against her hair. 'The night's made for other things.' He tilted back her head and kissed her full and passionately on the mouth. Her response was instant—he had been so right when he said her body was highly inflammable, but it had to be he who struck the match . . . She let him go on kissing her, let him undo the buttons of her blouse. Their bodies were so close she knew how much he too was roused and at any moment she expected him to carry her across to the bed and complete what he had started.

Instead, he broke away from her with a groan and said with an agonised wryness, 'Fay, forget about going away tomorrow. Stay here. Marry me.'

'What?' She couldn't believe her ears. 'Marry you? Me? But—but why? Sondra said you—and she——'

'I don't give a damn what Sondra said,' he interrupted violently. 'I'm asking you to marry me, Fay Douglas. I have no doubt it's irrational, ill-advised—all those things. I don't have any illusions about you or what I can expect from you. You're just another woman.'

Fay flinched at the phrase. 'Then—then why me?' Her senses were reeling and, madly, part of her longed to say yes in spite of everything. Physically they attracted each other, though for her it was far more than that. She was deeply in love with Dain, though so far she had held back her feelings and refused to let them flower. But once they were married, once he knew that the things he believed of her simply weren't true, mightn't she become more to him than just another woman?

He said with a darkly brooding look, 'Why you? Because I feel sure you and I will at least satisfy each other in bed. Will that do? And because I need a wife to bear my children. Would you be prepared to do that?'

'Yes,' she said unsteadily. Against all reason she was unbearably tempted.

'Then you agree?'

She shook her head helplessly. 'Why should I?'

'You know damned well why—your feminine logic will have told you that. Do you really want to go and work in some art shop when you can be here in bed with me, letting me do what you want me to do every time I touch you?'

She bit her lip, her cheeks scarlet. He talked as if she thought of nothing but sex, and she hated him for that. She hated him too because she knew she was going to say yes to his proposal. It would be the craziest gamble of her life, but the fact was she loved him as much as she hated him, despite the fact he was so hard, so cynical, so without belief. They would be marrying for passion and that was bad. But oh, how badly she wanted him, and how badly she wanted him to love her, to believe in her.

She said faintly, 'I wish you'd believe one thing, Dain——'

'What's that?'

'That Tony Thorpe was never my lover.'

He smiled cryptically. 'Why keep pushing that barrow, Fay? You know I'll find you out soon enough. But if you want it that way, then let's pretend you're the little virgin you presumably were when your mother went away. Let's just not talk about your very recent past.'

'All right,' she said unwillingly, her eyes falling before the look in his.

'You can come out with me after the sheep tomorrow,' she heard him say. And then he had gone.

He woke her in the morning knocking on her door, and Fay dragged herself out of a deep pool of sleep to come slowly and bewilderingly conscious. Around the room she saw the piles of clothes she had been packing last night and remembered what she had promised Dain: that she would marry him. It just didn't seem possible. Oh God, what had she done this time? It was the crowning effort of her current lunacy, and Sondra would be ropeable. Heaven knew what further lies she would tell Dain to break it up. And Sondra was coming today to take her to Canberra. Well, she wouldn't be here; she'd be way out in some paddock with Dain and the dogs and the sheep. It would be too bad for Sondra.

Yet, fatalistically, she knew that she couldn't win. So did she care?

She slithered out of bed and reached for her robe. Outside in the garden, the grass was shimmering in the early morning sunlight. She could hear a butcher bird calling sweetly, and her nerves tingled with excitement. She was learning to love it here and—yes, she did care, she wanted it, all of it, and most of all she wanted Dain Legend's love.

She knew it irrevocably when she joined Dain in the kitchen where he was grilling chops and bacon. This was where she wanted to spend the rest of her life—at Legend's Run, struggling to persuade him to love her. If you could persuade someone to love you, to trust you.

He said nothing of their talk last night, and if he remembered that Sondra was coming today he didn't mention it. Neither did Fay.

Breakfast over, they were soon riding away from the homestead together, Dain's kelpies, Kelly and Belle, trotting along behind the horses. The grass steamed gently in the sunshine, and Fay could almost see it growing—a film of green, shimmering over earth that had been dead and brown only days ago. The creek was racing madly and the leaves of the gum trees sparkled, and she felt a surge of sheer happiness swamp any doubts she might have had about what she was doing.

Soon Dain had to lean down from his horse to open a gate and they rode through kangaroo grass into a gully with timbered slopes where sheep were grazing. Dain pointed to a distant fence up on the skyline.

'Once we've mustered the sheep in this paddock the dogs will drive them through the gate into the far paddock and up on to the slopes.'

A little to her disappointment, he didn't give Fay any particular task to do, but let her ride with him while he directed the eager kelpies to hunt the sheep from the timber and gather them on the flats. There were no problems—which was probably why he had let her come. Soon the dogs were running round the wings of a smallish mob, driving the sheep in the direction of the far gate—urging them through, to funnel out on to the higher ground on the other side.

Glancing at Dain as she rode beside him, Fay wished they had a better understanding. If she lived here, she would come to love Legend's Run as he did. She'd want sons too. They'd have a wonderful life, a wonderful marriage. Or they could have, if only——

As it was, she could have no real faith in their future. It was all no more than a fantasy, a ball of thistledown that would blow away the minute Sondra clapped her hands.

Not long after noon, they started riding back towards the homestead. In spite of her enjoyment of the morning, Fay was tired, and it was a relief to know they wouldn't be out all day. But soon she remembered Sondra and her spirits plummeted. With foolish optimism she had imagined she wouldn't see Sondra today, but now she was far from sure about that, and sure enough, after they had crossed the creek, she saw the brilliant colour of Sondra's car gleaming among the trees near the homestead.

Dain saw it too and remarked dryly, 'I see Sondra's come to pick you up. We've certainly got a surprise for her!'

It was the first reference he had made to his proposal of last night, and Fay said hesitantly, 'If—if you want to change your mind about me, Dain, I mean—last night you were——'

'I was carried away?' he suggested. 'Well, I always am when I get too close to you. But I'm not changing my mind, Fay, and neither are you changing yours. What's the matter, anyhow? Are you afraid of Sondra?'

She was, of course. Because she was an intruder here. She and her mother were, like Tony Thorpe, fortune-hunters. That was how Sondra saw them, and when she came to think of it, it could look like that in her case.

Near the homestead, she and Dain dismounted and Martin, who was in charge of the stables, took over the horses. On shaking legs Fay followed Dain through the garden. At the house Sondra sat, obviously smouldering, on the verandah and Fay was aware, from the flicker in her grey-green eyes, that she was disconcerted that they had come back together. She hadn't been expecting to have him to contend with—but she'd manage. It would take a lot to baffle Sondra.

She pulled herself together very quickly and getting up came towards them with a smile.

'Why, hello, Dain! I didn't expect to see you. I came to see Fay about——' She stopped and looked at Fay significantly. 'You did tell Dain what you'd decided, didn't you, Fay?'

Fay bit her lip. Certainly she had told Dain—and Dain had agreed to her going. But things had happened after that——

She realised she hadn't replied to Sondra as Dain said, 'If you're talking about Fay going back to Canberra, Sondra, that's all off. She's staying here. We're going to be married.'

Fay caught her breath. How abrupt could you be! She saw Sondra recoil, blink with shock and then, miraculously, she recovered.

'Well! Congratulations to you both,' she exclaimed with a brilliant smile. 'I won't pretend I'm not surprised. I had no idea this was in the air. Is it going to be a long engagement?'

'Most definitely not.' Dain was already moving towards the door as if there were nothing more to be said about a not very important matter. 'I'll get some beer. Are you going to have lunch with us, Sondra?'

'I'd love to,' Sondra said. She was still smiling, but once he had disappeared her expression changed. 'You little *bitch*!' she snapped viciously. 'How did you work this? I told you I wanted you off Legend's Run. Are you pregnant—or pretending to be?'

Fay's face went dead white and she swallowed. 'Of course not! And I didn't—work it.'

'Oh dear, no!' Sondra sneered, nostrils dilating. 'I can guess the kind of thing that went on. I know your tactics—you'll have been falling all over him just the way you did with Tony when you imagined Confetti Downs was some sort of a showplace instead of a run-down dump.' She turned away to light a cigarette and Fay saw how her hands were shaking. 'But don't think you're getting away with it, that's all.'

Fay looked at her helplessly. 'But Sondra, don't you see? It's no use—Dain can't want to marry you or he'd never have——'

'Never have what?' Sondra was looking at her again, hatred plain in her eyes. 'If he's made love to you, it's because you were here and you encouraged it. I'm not a fool. I'm not a fool. I know it's not always the man who makes the running.'

As she spoke they heard Dain coming back and no more was said. Sondra resumed a pleasant expression and when they went in to lunch later she showed no signs of disturbance. The engagement wasn't mentioned again; Sondra talked about her work and its successful accomplishment, and then about the rain and the lovely green feed that was appearing in the paddocks. 'Let's hope we don't get too many more hot days that will burn it off,' she said knowledgeably. 'I guess you're doing a bit of reshuffling now to make the most of it.'

The talk went on, with Fay playing a decidedly minor part, until, as soon as the meal was over, Dain excused himself, saying he had to get back to work.

'I'll see you at dinner,' he told Fay before he took his departure. She half expected Sondra to go too, but when they left the table Sondra went on to the verandah with her and sat down.

'You've been too clever for me, Fay,' she remarked, lighting a cigarette. 'I guess I'll have to admit defeat.' Fay nearly fell over with surprise, and aware of her expression, Sondra grimaced before going on frankly, 'I don't like you, Fay. I wish you and your mother had never come into my life and turned everything upside down. I think Dain's made a big mistake to be taken in by you and I hope he comes to his senses before it's too late. Meanwhile, suppose we call a truce.'

She paused and Fay nodded, hardly able to believe what she heard.

'I was wondering if you could move your car out of the garage at the apartments,' Sondra went on. 'I intend staying in Canberra for a while and I don't want to leave my car in the street. If you let me have the keys I'll shift it myself—or would you rather bring it out here?'

Fay hesitated. It would be handy to have her car at Legend's Run, but she didn't see how she could get it. She said, 'I'd bring it here if Dain wasn't so busy. But I can hardly expect him to take time off to drive me to Canberra just now.'

'I suppose not,' Sondra agreed. 'But look—I'll be going to Canberra tomorrow. I can pick you up and you can get your car and do what you like with it, so long as it's out of my way.'

'Thank you,' Fay said uncertainly. 'I'll—I'll speak to Dain about it tonight and see what he says.'

'He's hardly likely to object,' Sondra said dryly. 'I shan't be going till the afternoon, though, I have other things to do in the morning.' She glanced at her watch. 'I'll be on my way, then. I'll see you tomorrow, shall I?'

'Yes. And—thank you,' said Fay with an effort.

'Don't thank me. It's for my benefit,' the other girl said indifferently. She moved to the verandah steps, then paused. 'If you have any shopping to do, you could stay in town overnight. I'm sure Dain would let you. I'll be moving into the apartment myself anyhow, so you won't be alone. And you really ought to go to the hairdresser, you know.'

Fay flushed slightly. 'I suppose so. I'll ask Dain.'

'You do that. Ask Dain,' said Sondra, the sour note back in her voice.

Fay watched her get into her car and drive away. She didn't blame her for being sour. It was rather frightful when some other girl came along and snatched up the man you loved—or wanted, she corrected herself. She didn't really think Sondra loved Dain. She had said she wanted him—and she wanted Legend's Run. Presently she wandered inside and in her room looked critically at herself in the mirror. It was true her hair needed trimming, but she didn't really want to stay the night in Canberra—with her stepsister. She went into the sitting room and telephoned the hairdresser—but found it was impossible to get an appointment for late the following afternoon. She made one instead for the morning after. She could cancel it if she came home.

She dressed up for dinner that night. After all, she and Dain had just become engaged and—oh well, why not be honest and admit to herself that she wanted to look her best for him? She put on the black skirt and the violet shirt, leaving the top buttons undone to show the curve of her breast.

When he came home it had started to rain again and the sound on the roof was pleasant. He showered and changed into dark pants and cream silk shirt. Mrs Lindsay left, leaving Fay to dish up the dinner, and Dain produced a bottle of white wine to go with the chicken casserole. He said nothing about their engagement, and if she had expected a toast when the wine was poured, it was not forthcoming.

Afterwards they sat on the verandah, the soft lamp-light reflected in the beautiful polished floor, the sound of the rain in the garden seeming to close them in together intimately. Dain had poured himself a Scotch and as he drank it, he looked at her. She had chosen to sit on the long cane couch, but he had taken a chair placed at an angle to it, and stretched his long legs out in front of him, looked at her over his glass and said nothing. It was unnerving, and after several minutes, Fay asked uneasily, 'Why are you looking at me like that?'

He raised one eyebrow. 'Because I've acquired you. And I'm wondering if I regret it.'

She bit her lip. 'I wish you wouldn't talk like that—as though I were a—a possession!'

'You are—or soon will be.' He added, 'A very beautiful and exquisite possession, Fay, as I'm well aware. But while the romantic in me admires your loveliness, the cynic reminds me that my—treasure has already been enjoyed by another man.'

'That's not true,' she protested, her blue eyes wide and appealing. 'I've tried to tell you, Dain——'

'Then stop trying.' He swallowed down the rest of his Scotch and set the crystal glass down on the table at his elbow. 'You look very pretty stretching your eyes like that and putting on your little act of innocence, but I've seen too many just such displays to be impressed. My wife was a pretty woman—she knew how to assume a virginal air.'

Fay felt despair engulf her. Was he always going to distrust her? If so—— She burst out, 'How can I possibly marry you when you're like that?'

He shrugged. 'I can only deduce that you're aware of the benefits attached.' His dark eyes roamed over her, lingering on her breast, exposed by the deep V of her neckline, then coming back to her face and connecting up with her own eyes.

Fay wanted to say, 'You're wrong, quite wrong. I don't care a fig about the benefits attached—it's just that I love you——' But what was the use? He'd never believe her. He'd make another of his hurtful statements. She felt herself go limp with misery. How could she go on with this? He would be better off with Sondra, who was worldly enough to take his cynical attitude in her stride. She would have to think about it—hard—before it was too late. Which somehow brought her back to tomorrow, so that when she spoke again it was to change the subject completely.

'I was going to ask you if you mind if I go in to Canberra tomorrow for my car. I'd—I'd like to go to the hairdressers too, and do some shopping.'

Dain looked at her through narrowed eyes. 'Go ahead. It's already arranged, I presume.'

'More or less,' she admitted. 'But I said I'd ask you about it. We—Sondra and I—won't be leaving till after lunch and I can't get an appointment with the hairdresser till the next morning. Sondra's staying at the apartment for a few days,' she continued carefully, 'so—so will it be all right if I stay in town overnight?'

'I suppose so,' he said. He got up from his chair and paced along the verandah and back, then stopped to stare down at her. 'If you're planning to walk out on me, Fay, you'd better tell me.'

'I'm not,' she said. She looked up at him and felt her heart begin to pound. Dain reached down suddenly, pulling her to her feet and into his arms. His mouth claimed hers and she felt desire for him spring to life as though at a magic word. It was insane, how quickly he could ignite her passion—and she knew it was the same with him. He held her closely to him, one hand against the small of her back, the other, her shirt pulled free of her skirt, caressing her bare skin.

'What do you think?' he said against the smoothness of her neck. 'Will you sleep in my bed tonight, Fay?'

She drew a shuddering breath. 'Do you want me to?'

'You would, wouldn't you?' he said, so cynically that she pulled away from him. What did he think she was? A—a whore? She must be mad to have fallen in love with him when his opinion of her was so abysmally low.

She asked him tightly, 'Why don't you believe in me, Dain?'

'Because I don't believe in any woman. I know too much about them.'

Fay sank down on the couch. What was the use? His opinion of her would go way down if she said she would sleep with him tonight—so far down that he would probably refuse her. And therein lay the paradox. Because he had only to make love to her to know that she was innocent. It seemed she had fallen off the edge of a cliff when she had fallen in love with him. Her marriage was going to be hell if she couldn't win him back from his cynicism. And how on earth was she to do that? For without it, she didn't have the heart to go ahead.

When they parted for the night, they had not even exchanged another kiss.

CHAPTER TEN

It was after four when Sondra arrived next afternoon. The rain had stopped and Fay had already taken her overnight case on to the verandah. 'So Dain's allowing you to stay in town,' Sondra remarked as she carried it out to the car.

They had little to say to each other during the drive. Sondra had heard from her father, but didn't offer any news about Claire. Fay volunteered the information that she had an appointment with the hairdresser next morning, and beyond that they seemed to have nothing to say to each other. Once at the apartment, Fay went straight to the garage to see if her car battery was flat.

'I suppose you'll want to garage your car right away,' she remarked as she got out of the car, but Sondra said casually, 'Oh, there's no great hurry. I have a dinner date tonight and I'm driving myself.'

While Fay checked her car, Sondra went up to the apartment, and presently Fay backed the Gemini out of the garage and parked it in the street, so that Sondra would be able to use the garage when she came home from her date.

When she went upstairs to the flat, Sondra was changing to go out. On the telephone table was a letter for Fay from her mother in Paris. It appeared she and Walter were having a wonderful time in spite of the cold. She gave a brief résumé of where they had been so far, and gave an address in Cannes to which Fay could write, as they would be staying there for several days. 'I hope Dain Legend has been keeping in touch with you,' the letter concluded, 'and that you haven't been giving him any trouble.' Fay made a face over that. What would her mother think when she knew they were going to be be married? She wondered if they would wait till Claire came back. Dain had told Sondra it wasn't going to be a long engagement, but he hadn't discussed dates at all with his bride-to-be.

She had gone to her bedroom to find notepaper and write a reply when Sondra came to her door looking very glamorous in a cream and gold silk chiffon dress, her blonde hair arranged in a new style up and away from her face, her make-up perfect.

'I'm going now, Fay. I'll see you in the morning.'

'Oh—yes. I've moved my car out of the garage, Sondra.'

Sondra nodded but didn't thank her, and a moment later Fay heard the front door click shut behind her.

It was strange to be back in the flat. Fay wandered round, switching on the lights and the television and looking into all the rooms. Sondra's room was neat and tidy, her clothes had all been put away, but on the dressing table her eye caught a silver gleam, and she discovered it was the key to the front door. Which meant, she thought irritably, that she would have to stay awake to let her stepsister in. She hoped she wasn't going to be too late home.

She fixed herself a meal from the freezer, then when she had washed her dishes she sank back in the sofa in the sitting room, the television on, her writing pad on her knees. She had taken her shoes off and was comfortable in an old pair of jeans and a T-shirt. It seemed a lifetime since she had been actually living here, and her mind flipped back to the evening when Dain had appeared—and found her entertaining a man in her flat. How long ago it seemed, and what a lot had happened since then! He had suspected the worst of her that very first time, she remembered. If he only knew how absolutely innocent her encounters with Tony had been, he would be absolutely stunned.

If only he did know, she repeated silently to herself. It would make a world of difference. Because he was attracted to her, just as she was attracted to him. And perhaps because he so easily stirred her passion he imagined Tony had done so too, and that she had given in to him. He was completely wrong about that.

She glanced down at the writing pad on her knee. What on earth was she going to say to her mother? 'Dain Legend has been keeping very closely in touch with me—so closely that we've decided to be married. And I've been giving him more trouble than you'd believe!'

Thinking of Dain made her restless, and she had the brilliant idea that she would ring him up. She had just got to her feet when the doorbell rang. Sondra already—and it wasn't yet nine o'clock!

But when she opened the door it was Tony Thorpe. She stared at him in surprise—that stunningly handsome man with the blue eyes and the white teeth. He was smiling at her now and she thought, 'Why on earth did I think he was so marvellous?' She could see the weakness in his face now, the emptiness in the eyes she had found so frank and open.

'I saw your light and thought I'd come up and see if it was you or Sondra,' he said. 'Are you going to ask me in, Fay?'

'Yes—come in, of course,' she said vaguely. She closed the door behind him and led the way into the sitting room. He looked around, then sat down on the sofa, moving her writing things so she could sit beside him.

'It's like old times, isn't it?' he remarked, and she gave him a wry look. She didn't sit near him but switched off the television and took one of the armchairs, and found she was wishing she hadn't invited him in after all. It was quite pointless.

'Before I forget,' he said, leaning forward and rooting in the pocket of the cream jacket he was wearing. 'The money I owe you.' He took a wad of notes from his wallet and held it out to her. 'Count it. It's every penny you lent me—plus the money for that hotel bill.'

Fay took it in silence. The notes were crisp and new and looked to be straight from the bank. She didn't count them, though Tony was watching her smilingly. While he did so, he removed his jacket and unbuttoned the top of his shirt, then stooped to loosen his shoes.

She said hastily, 'Thank you for returning the money, Tony. I'd rather you didn't stay, though.'

'Now, Fay!' he exclaimed. 'You know you can trust me. Couldn't we have a cup of coffee and I'll try to explain why I behaved so rottenly.'

'You've already explained,' she said. 'And I do understand. But I'd—I'd rather you went now.'

'You're not scared of being alone with me! Come on, Fay, let me make the coffee, then—I really could do with a cup.'

She gave in reluctantly because there seemed nothing else to do. 'All right. But then you must go. Sondra will be back soon anyhow.' She went into the kitchen to make the coffee while he stayed in the sitting room making himself very much at home. 'How do you get rid of someone like Tony?' she wondered worriedly. She didn't want him there when Sondra came in. Moreover, she didn't want to hear any more explanations from him. He could explain his behaviour for a million years and she would never accept it. He had pretended to feel more for her than he had. What had appealed to him all the time was Walter Marshall's money, just as Dain had said, and he couldn't convince her otherwise.

When she carried the coffee in to the sitting room, he had taken off his shoes and switched on the television, turning to a channel that was showing an old thriller movie.

'That was a great show,' he said from the depths of the sofa. 'Did you ever see it, Fay?'

'Yes,' she said, and added coolly, 'But I don't want to see it again.'

He ignored her, took the cup of coffee she handed him, and leaning back watched the show.

Fay began to feel both frightened and angry. How dared he impose on her like this? The minute he had finished his coffee she was going to switch off the television and tell him to go. Perhaps Sondra would come back. She hoped so. It was the first time in her life she had actually longed for her stepsister to put in an appearance.

Tony finished his coffee, and she stood up at once and said firmly, 'You must go now, Tony.' She switched the television off, then turned to face him, and found he was still leaning back on the sofa. 'Please put your shoes on and go, Tony.'

He grimaced, but he got up. 'All right. But I'd like to use the loo first.' He vanished in the direction of the bathroom, and with a sigh of relief Fay gathered up the cups and saucers and took them to the kitchen. She washed them up, dried them and put them away and then stood listening uneasily. She hadn't heard the bathroom door open, and she felt too embarrassed to call out to Tony.

After a moment she went back to the sitting room, picked up her writing pad and ballpoint and looked at what she had so far written—'Dear Mother, It was lovely to hear from you——' She couldn't think of a single thing to write beyond that, she was so much on edge. She stared at Tony's shoes sprawling on the floor and wished he would come and put them on and go.

At last she could stand it no longer, and she went into the hall and called clearly, 'Are you all right, Tony?'

There was no reply for a moment, then the door opened and he emerged. He said with a groan, 'I feel crook—I've got to lie down.' He staggered through the nearest door which happened to be Fay's room, and collapsed on the bed. Fay hurried in after him, filled with anxiety.

'What's the matter, Tony? Where do you feel bad? Is it your stomach?'

'Must be something I ate,' he said with another groan, hunching his knees up and looking at her in the half dark.

'Oh dear,' Fay said worriedly. She switched on the reading lamp and he flung his arm across his face and turned away from it. 'I'd better call the doctor. It's not appendicitis, is it? Where's the pain?'

'Oh, it's general. Don't make a big thing of it. It's something I ate—I had some oysters in a crummy little restaurant. Get me some Alka-Seltzer or something— and maybe if I could have a sleep——'

'You'll have to—to move out of here,' she said, hesitating. 'Into the sitting room or——'

'Okay,' he said. 'But just get me something first.'

Fay hurried away to get the Alka-Seltzer, but before she had even poured water into the glass, the doorbell rang. Thank goodness—it must be Sondra, she thought. But when she opened the front door she found it was Dain standing there.

Her cheeks flamed and then grew pale.

'I—I thought it was Sondra,' she said faintly as he brushed past her and moved along the hallway towards the sitting room.

'Now why would you think that?' he wondered.

'Sondra's out at the cottage. She had no intention of staying in town. She called in at the homestead when she came back from her dinner date to see if you'd arrived home safely.'

'But—but she can't have,' Fay said helplessly. 'She *is* staying here——'

He had reached the sitting room now and her heart sank as he looked at Tony's shoes on the floor, his jacket on the sofa—the tumbled cushions, the low lights.

'History repeating itself,' he said, his voice harsh. 'Who is it?'

'It's—it's Tony Thorpe,' she faltered. 'He came to return the money he owed me and now he's—he's not feeling well. He's lying down——'

He believed her, she thought with relief, seeing the change in his expression, but her relief was shortlived. Dain's eyes had moved past her now and she turned her head slowly. Tony had appeared and to her horror and bewilderment he said with a lazy smile, 'Come on, Fay, what's the use of pretending? We're not kids, either of us, and if we——'

The next instant Dain's arm had swung out, Tony staggered, then crashed to the floor.

Fay darted forward with a little cry, but he was already getting hastily to his feet.

'Get out of here before I hit you again,' Dain gritted. 'No, on second thoughts I'll come with you.' He sent Fay a look of such blazing anger that she shrank back from him, her throat dry.

'I don't want a fight,' Tony said sullenly. He wiped blood from the corner of his mouth with the back of his hand, then moved across the room to put his feet into his shoes and reach for his jacket.

Somehow Fay found her voice and protested shakily, 'Why did you say that, Tony? You know I'm telling the truth. You were sick, and——' Her voice broke off. What a fool she was! Of course he wasn't sick! Her eyes widened at the realisation, and she said slowly, 'You were pretending. But—but why?'

'Oh, quit trying to wriggle out of it, Fay,' he muttered, shrugging into his coat and sending Dain a quick wary look. 'You invited me for the night. It wasn't all my idea.'

Fay gasped. 'That's a lie!' She too looked at Dain, who stood staring first at Tony, then at her, his eyes narrowed, his nostrils white. He looked as if he would like to kill both of them, and right now she wanted to die. 'Do you believe him?' she demanded, her voice shaking. 'Because if you do, then I'm through with you, Dain Legend! I could never marry a man who had no trust in me. I—I don't want ever to see you again—not ever!'

She burst into tears and fled to her room, slammed the door and flung herself face down on the bed sobbing heartbrokenly. She heard raised voices—a few thuds—a heavier one—then she subsided into her own misery.

Why had Tony lied? What did he have against her? It was all so pointless ... Then suddenly she realised—Sondra was at the back of it, of course. She had to be. She knew Tony was in Canberra again—she must have rigged this thing somehow, planned it all. Sondra with her hobnailed boots. And Dain, who had no faith in women, was going to swallow it. Oh, she'd been an idiot to let herself fall in love with him. He didn't love her, that was obvious. Well, it was all over now. She wasn't going to marry him. She'd meant it when she said she never wanted to see him again. She would leave Canberra, start again somewhere else now she had her savings back.

She sat up and dried her eyes and listened intently.

She couldn't hear a thing. Had they gone, both of them? She hoped so. She felt exhausted, and her life was empty——

Her eyes filled with tears so that when the bedroom door opened and Dain appeared she saw him through a blur.

'Go—away,' she said brokenly.

He took no notice, but came into the room and sat down on the bed. 'I'm sorry, Fay,' he said, his voice low.

She blinked her tears away and stared at him. Dain Legend was sorry! She must be dreaming. She gave a laugh that was half a sob and repeated, 'You're sorry! But—but what for?' She knew it was no use telling herself she never wanted to see him again. She did—and like a fool, she supposed she'd forgive him for anything. But only—only because she loved him—crazily.

'I'm sorry for more things than I can ever tell you, Fay,' he said, his dark eyes totally serious. 'I'm not fit to come near you——'

'Don't say that,' she said weakly. 'But what's happened? Where's Tony? Did you——'

'He's still in one piece—just about. And he's gone.'

She swallowed. 'Do you still believe what he said?'

'I believe what I've just forced out of him,' he said grimly. He had reached for one of her hands and he held it in both of his. 'I've been a swine, Fay, all along. I know I can't expect you to marry me now. You must think I'm a monster——'

She looked at him—his dark hair, his unshaven jaw, the sensual curve of his mouth. It wasn't cruel now, it was—sad. She had never seen him look sad before—bitter, cynical, cruel. But never sad, and she had an almost irresistible impulse to put her lips against his and kiss him. He wasn't a monster—for her he could never be that. As for marrying him——

He raised his eyes to hers. 'There's something I've

never told you, Fay.'

'What?' she whispered.

'That I love you.'

Her eyes widened incredulously, her heart beat hard and the bright colour flowed into her cheeks and away again. 'But—but you can't——' she said insanely.

'Can't I? I can't help it,' he said. 'I've been fighting against it for long enough, but it's no use. I swore long ago I'd never love a woman again—never be fool enough to trust any female. And I haven't trusted you, to my shame. I've behaved like a brute, but oh God, I haven't been able to stop myself falling in love with you. And you must hate me.'

Fay shook her head, then said honestly, 'Only when you refused to believe me ... What did Tony tell you just now? I don't understand——'

'Tony told me several things,' he said grimly. 'I threatened to beat him up if he wouldn't talk. It's as well you got out of the room, Fay. He finally admitted he'd been offered a large sum of money to come here tonight—to stay till I arrived, to let me think he'd been making love to you——'

Sondra, Fay thought. So she had been right. And the large sum of money—that would have been the money Sondra should have used to pay the furniture bill. It certainly would have been well worth Tony's while to do what she wanted!

'I suppose you can guess who planned it all,' Dain said wearily, and Fay nodded. She didn't think either she or Dain would be seeing much of Sondra Marshall in future. 'She's the woman I shouldn't have trusted, not you,' he admitted.

'I'm sorry,' Fay said.

'Have you anything to be sorry about?'

She nodded. 'Going away with Tony in the first place. I—I really wanted you to stop me, but you didn't. I didn't know you'd had to go away. Sondra didn't tell me. I don't really know why I did it. I—I tried to fall in love with Tony, but it didn't work. I guess I must have been half in love with you even then.'

'And now—are you still half in love with me, darling?' His voice was urgent as he drew her into his arms and looked deeply into her eyes.

For answer she raised her lips to his. Their lips met, fire ran through her veins.

'Make love to me, Dain,' she whispered against his mouth, and he pulled her down on the bed beside him.

SAVE TIME, TROUBLE & MONEY!
By joining the exciting NEW...

Mills & Boon Romance CLUB

WITH all these EXCLUSIVE BENEFITS for every member

NOTHING TO PAY! MEMBERSHIP IS FREE TO REGULAR READERS!

IMAGINE the *pleasure* and *security* of having ALL your favourite *Mills & Boon* romantic fiction delivered right to *your* home, absolutely POST FREE... straight off the press! No waiting! No more disappointments! All this PLUS all the latest news of *new books* and *top-selling authors* in your own monthly MAGAZINE... PLUS *regular* big CASH SAVINGS... PLUS lots of wonderful strictly-limited, *members-only* SPECIAL OFFERS! All these exclusive benefits can be yours – right NOW – simply by joining the exciting NEW *Mills & Boon* ROMANCE CLUB. Complete and post the coupon below for FREE full-colour leaflet. It costs nothing. HURRY!

No obligation to join unless you wish!

FREE CLUB MAGAZINE Packed with advance news of latest titles and authors

Exciting offers of **FREE BOOKS** For club members ONLY

Lots of fabulous **BARGAIN OFFERS** – many at **BIG CASH SAVINGS**

FREE FULL-COLOUR LEAFLET!
CUT OUT CUT OUT COUPON BELOW AND POST IT TODAY!

To: **MILLS & BOON READER SERVICE, P.O. Box No 236, Thornton Road, Croydon, Surrey CR9 3RU, England.**
WITHOUT OBLIGATION to join, please send me FREE details of the exciting NEW Mills & Boon ROMANCE CLUB and of all the exclusive benefits of membership.

Please write in BLOCK LETTERS below

NAME (Mrs/Miss) ....

ADDRESS ....

CITY/TOWN ....

COUNTY/COUNTRY.................... POST/ZIP CODE..................

Readers in South Africa and Zimbabwe please write to:
P.O. BOX 1872, Johannesburg, 2000. S. Africa